FORGOTTEN PLANS

Forgotten Plans

ISBN: (hardback)
(paperback)
(ebook)

Printed in the United States of America

FORGOTTEN PLANS

A Jeannie Loomis Novel

GARY J. ROSE

ALSO, BY THE AUTHOR:

Towards the Integration of Police Psychology Techniques to Combat Juvenile Delinquency in K-12 Classrooms

Hitting Rock Bottom

Teaching Inside the Walls

How to Create a Public-School Military Style Boot Camp Academy

Ark of the Covenant – Raid on the Church of Our Lady Mary of Zion
(A Jeannie Loomis Novel)

Star Chamber
(A Jeannie Loomis Novel)

For Mike Lake and his canine companion Ripley

Mom

My daughter Mandy

"The great enemy of writing is interruption."

—Joyce Carol Oates

PREFACE

Osama bin Laden, al-Qaeda leader and the world's most hunted terrorist, was responsible for numerous terrorist attacks against the United States and other Western powers, including the U.S. warship Cole suicide bombing in the Yemeni port of Aden in 2000, and the World Trade Center and Pentagon attacks on September 11, 2001. Shortly thereafter he issued two *fatwas* (Arabic: "religious opinions") declaring a holy war against the United States which he accused of looting the Muslim world's natural resources, occupying the Arabian Peninsula and the holy sites of Islam, and supporting governments servile to U.S. interests in the Middle East, among other things. He subsequently released audio messages including a 2008 threat to retaliate for Palestinian deaths in the Gaza Strip, and a 2009 challenge directed at the new U.S. president, Barack Obama, to continue the fight against al-Qaeda. Bin Laden was located and killed on May 2, 2011. Several days after Obama's announcement that bin Laden was dead, al-Qaeda released a statement publicly acknowledging his death and vowing revenge.

Shortly before the al-Qaeda leader was killed, he released a final audio message from his compound in Abbottabad, Pakistan. In the message, bin Laden praised the Tunisian and Egyptian uprisings in early September 2011 and called on al-Qaeda followers to help people struggling against unjust governments. Osama bin Laden also secretively issued three new *fatwas* declaring that the holy war against the United States must be accelerated. He envisioned an event that would not only shock the world, but strike another dagger into the heart of America: an event that would surpass the number of deaths resulting from the 9-11 attacks.

THEN

OPERATION NEPTUNE SPEAR
MAY 1, 2011 – MAY 2, 2011

Abbottabad, Pakistan is located 34 miles from the capital, Islamabad. Two and a half-miles north-east of the city center stood a three-story compound at the end of a narrow dirt road. Built in 2004 on a plot of land eight times larger than nearby houses was a main structure surrounded by a 12-to-18-foot concrete wall topped with barbed wire and two security gates. The third-floor balcony was surrounded by a seven-foot high privacy wall tall enough to hide the world's most wanted terrorist: 6 feet 4-inch Osama bin Laden. It was this compound that Navy SEALs using the code name Operation Neptune Spear raided during the night of May 1, 2011 and the early morning hours of May 2, 2011, killing bin Laden and confiscating his cache of computers and technology related items.

President Obama met with the National Security Council on March 14 to review possible options for raiding the compound. He was concerned that the mission would be exposed and he wanted to proceed quickly. For that reason, he ruled out Pakistani involvement.

Defense Secretary Robert Gates and other military officials expressed doubts as to whether the individual seen on drone flyovers was indeed bin Laden and questioned whether a commando raid was worth the risk. Weighing the other option of dropping 32, 2,000-pound bombs fitted with a JDAM guidance system and unknown collateral damage, Obama directed Admiral McRaven to fully develop a helicopter raid. Finally, after intense simulated raids, Obama was told that the squad was ready. On April 29 at 8:20 a.m. EDT, Obama gave the go-ahead for Operation Neptune Spear. Unfortunately, the plan had to be delayed one day due to cloudy weather.

The SEALs flew into Pakistan from a base in Jalalabad. The U.S. Army Special Operation Command Unit known as the "Night Stalkers" provided two modified Black Hawk helicopters, as well as larger Chinook heavy-lift helicopters employed as backups. These specially equipped helicopters using previously unseen "stealth" technology flew more quietly, and were harder to detect on radar than conventional models. Due to the extra weight of the stealth equipment in the Black Hawks, cargo was calculated to the ounce with the weather factored in. The raid was scheduled for a time with little moonlight so the helicopters could enter Pakistan low to the ground and undetected. The flight from Jalalabad to Abbottabad took about 90 minutes.

After Osama bin Laden was located and killed, his clothing was examined and found to contain 500 Euros, and two phone numbers sewn into the fabric. Bin Laden's body was taken by the SEALs; however, dead combatants were left behind. The defenders secured each floor and individuals within the compound, and then moved carefully through the rooms--collecting ten computers, hard drives, numerous DVDs, almost one-hundred thumb drives, more than a dozen cell phones, and other electronic equipment for analysis. Due to the destruction of one operational helicopter, one of the two Chinooks held in reserve arrived at the compound to rescue the SEALs and take bin Laden's body out of Pakistan. His body was later buried at sea.

The material gathered at the compound by the SEAL team was stored at the FBI Laboratory in

Quantico, Virginia, and copies of it were provided to agencies needing to preserve a chain of custody as evidence for any future trial. Some of the documents revealed that bin Laden had stayed in touch with al-Qaeda's established affiliates, and that he sought new alliances with groups such as Boko Haram from Nigeria. He sought to reassert control over loosely affiliated jihadist factions from Yemen to Somalia, as well as independent actors whom he believed had sullied al-Qaeda's reputation and muddied its central message. Bin Laden was worried about his personal security and was annoyed that his organization had not utilized the Arab Spring to improve his image. Other materials showed that bin Laden was a "hands-on" manager who participated in the terrorist group's operational planning and strategic thinking, while also giving orders and advice to field operatives scattered worldwide. In a few documents, bin Laden stated that al-Qaeda's strength was limited, and therefore the best way to attack the U.S.--which he compared to a tree--was, "to concentrate on sawing the trunk." He wanted to extend and develop operations in America, and not be limited to blowing-up airplanes.

Bin Laden debated the possible assassination of President Obama when/if Obama was traveling with David Petraeus to Pakistan and Afghanistan. An opportunity did present itself in the travel agenda for Vice President Biden, but bin Laden felt this would not be worthwhile since "Biden was totally unprepared for the post of president and if he was elected president, would self-destruct and damage the U.S. without no help needed from al-Qaeda." He also stated that he was against one-person suicide attacks and was of the opinion that at least two individuals should undertake attacks instead.

The CIA eventually released over 470,000 documents confiscated in the bin Laden raid. In addition to the nearly half-million documents confiscated, there were the al-Qaeda leader's personal journal, his home movies, and a rare video of his son's wedding in addition to audio files, images, videos, and software operating system files.

Of greatest interest to the CIA was a file in which bin Laden discussed al-Qaeda's 2011 preparations to commemorate the 10th anniversary of the 9/11 Trade Center attacks, efforts to exploit the "Arab Awakening" in the Middle East, and efforts to promote global jihad. Potential targets were listed; however, no single target appeared to have been selected.

Due to the enormous amount of intelligence contained in the computer hard drives and thumb drives, priority was placed on items that had been encrypted. Non-encrypted laptop and software material was placed in a secure location for later examination. One of the unencrypted laptops contained information listing three of Bin Laden's selected targets to be destroyed pending his death.

NOW

"Two-step" closed his eyes, and kept them shut for 15-seconds before entering a Market Street, San Francisco bar. Employing the "shut-eye" technique he learned in Vietnam prepared his eyes to adjust to the darkness he would soon experience inside the tavern.

The bar was nothing extravagant. It was first built and used as a general merchandise establishment, but rebuilt following the 1909 San Francisco earthquake which demolished most of the two-story structure. Its function had changed many times over the years: street side grocery outlet, laundry, Chinese restaurant, private men's club, two upscale pubs, and now an average drinking establishment. This afternoon there were a few patrons nursing beers and eating beer nuts. Two males were sitting next to each other at the bar. There were no barmaids that he could see, but the bartender recognized him from a few previous visits and asked if he wanted his usual.

"No," Two-step replied. "Bring me a pitcher of dark beer and four glasses instead. I have friends meeting me here. Got any nachos yet?"

"I'm just warming up the cheese. When do you expect your friends?

"Should be here any minute. Just bring a bunch when they arrive. Thanks."

Blackbeard arrived first. Standing 5'8," he weighed around 165 pounds and sported a full dark black beard. He was given the nickname because of his resemblance to the infamous pirate, Edward Teach, known as Blackbeard. Teach and other pirates plagued shipping lanes off North America and throughout the Caribbean in the early-eighteenth century, and he was known as the most notorious of all sea robbers.

Blackbeard walked over to the corner booth where Two-step was seated. They gave each other high-fives, and turned to the opening front door through which Apache, the third member of the crew, entered. Apache appeared to have no problem adjusting to the dimly lit room, having served in the Vietnam tunnels like Two-step. His right shirt-sleeve rode up when he stretched across the table to shake hands with Two-step and Blackbeard, displaying the tattoo of a rat holding a revolver in one hand and a flashlight in the other. He grabbed a mug and began pouring himself a beer.

"So, how's it hanging, dudes?" he asked.

"Can't fuckin complain, since no one gives a shit anyway," Blackbeard said while looking at the other two. "You still seeing that chick from the diner? What's her name, Anita?" he asked, looking at Apache.

"No, she found some asshole who had more money than me and split. Good riddance, I say. How about you? You gettin' any?" he asked.

"Nay, porn is all the excitement I'm getting," Blackbeard said while laughing. "At least I won't get any STDs."

The door opened and another male entered. He was short and skinny, had a pale complexion and blond hair, and sported acid-wash Levi's and a red hoodie. He stood for several seconds behind the now closed entrance door, trying to adjust to the limited illumination of the bar. Unlike Two-step and Apache, Jimmy had no experience in the military; but he did have tunnel experience in Virginia's coal mines like the other two.

"Two-step, Blackbeard, Apache; how the hell have you assholes been?" Jimmy asked as he bump-fisted each one.

Each gave his own verbal answer of "not bad" or "could be worse," while Two-step passed a mug and the pitcher of beer. He got the bartender's attention and ordered another pitcher, adding that the bartender could send the nachos when ready.

"Nachos? Great, I'm starving," Jimmy said. "Do they have anything else besides nachos?"

"The barmaid will bring pizzas when she comes in, and I'll have her bring some over. Is that OK with you kid?" Two-step asked with a smile.

"Bitchin," Jimmy said. "So, what's up that brings us all together again…another job?" Jimmy asked.

Two-step waited with his reply until the bartender delivered four dishes loaded with cheese-covered chips to the table, then brought another pitcher of beer from the bar. "Let me know if you need anything else," he said. "We'll take at least one whole pizza when Linda gets in," Two-step said. "You got it," the retreating bartender responded.

Two-step pulled a couple of folded papers from his Levi's' rear pocket and started to lay them out. He, too, was sporting a tattoo on his arm of a rat with a gun in one hand and a flashlight in the other—almost identical to Apache's. He and Apache had been Tunnel Rats during the Vietnam conflict, and after getting drunk one night in Saigon they both got the now famous Tunnel Rat engraving on their arms. Two-step was given his nickname in recognition of an extremely poisonous snake they sometimes encountered clearing out VC tunnels in the bush. The small snakes were sometimes called "Two-step Charlies" because of the erroneous myth that a person bitten by one was likely to die within two steps. GIs knew this was not true although the snake, believed to be a many-banded Krait, was highly venomous.

Apache was a full-blooded North American native and bragged that his bloodline could be traced back to Geronimo. No one ever questioned him about that. He and Two-step met in Vietnam and became Tunnel Rats within two-weeks of each other. Two-step owed Apache his life after Apache pulled him from a tunnel collapse a month before they were both slated to get out of the army. Apache always downplayed what he had done, saying that Two-step would have done the same for him--which was probably true.

Everyone leaned forward and stared at the papers. "What is it?" Jimmy asked. Jimmy was the youngest of the group, having met Blackbeard in West Virginia where they had worked together as coal miners. Blackbeard only weighed 150 pounds back then, but once he gave up smoking, he shot-up to his present weigh. Both of them left the coal mining profession for more lucrative work with Two-step, albeit criminal in nature. Jimmy was the thinnest of the group. Two-step suspected he used meth since Jimmy's teeth looked like that found on a carved Halloween pumpkin, but he was always reliable.

Rearranging and pointing to a specific spot on one of the papers, Two-step said, "This is our next tunnel job--the Bank of America in San Francisco located here on Market and Van Ness, right across from where we're sitting." He took the second piece of paper, placed it on top of the first and continued: "And, this is the underground sewer system for that section of the city. According to a reliable source, the bank's been having a lot of problems with its alarm system. Every time management is assured it's fixed, it misfires and triggers another alarm. The bank and assistant managers are getting pissed-off at repeatedly having to come and see if everything's alright, and once again waiting for the monitoring service to reset it. From now until the day we blow the bank, Christmas Day, we'll occasionally set off the alarm at different nightly hours; hopefully, they'll not respond to the bank on Christmas or be half-assed in doing it."

Jimmy asked, "How are you setting off the alarm?"

"I learned that the bank's motion-detector alarm system is super-sensitive. I set up near the bank, and using a pulse gun I aimed it at anything I could see in the bank's interior. The alarm isn't triggered when the doors are rattled, but as soon as any item in the bank's main area moves--bang! Off goes the alarm. Lately, while monitoring responses, I've noticed that neither the cops nor the bank management enters the bank--they just glance inside instead. As you can see from these diagrams, we'll have to tunnel (pointing to a spot on the paper) to here: approximately 75-feet which will place us right under the vault floor." Two-step stopped and looked at everyone to see if he had a buy-in.

"We'll need to get rid of a lot of dirt and debris, but no one from the city seems to ever go down into this sewer area unless there's a rainstorm back-up. If we can blow a connecting tunnel to this section of the sewer, we can simply transfer the dirt over there--saving time and reducing our exposure to the outside while we tunnel.

We'll pretty much use the same plan as our last job with Blackbeard, placing the shape-charges here, here, and here under the vault floor (again, pointing to the diagram). We set-off another alarm and wait for the cops and bank staff to respond. After they leave, we wait about 40-minutes and then set-off the blast. This might set-off the alarm, so we'll wait and see if anyone responds. I doubt it, but we'll see." Two-step waited for questions or comments, but got none.

"When I feel it's safe, we'll all climb up into the vault and drill all of the safety-deposit box locks without removing the boxes themselves that time."

"Why is that?" Jimmy asked.

"It'll save time," said Apache. "Last time, if you guys remember, we left several boxes untouched due to time. I mean, everyone took time to drill the two locks on each box then opened them to look inside, and it slowed us down. This way, once the locks are destroyed, we can quickly throw all the contents onto the vault floor--well, what remains of the floor--and sort through the valuables." He nodded at Two-step to see if he was correct in his assessment, and got a "correct" answer in return.

"That's the plan. Any questions?" asked Two-step.

"Is your 'reliable source' that plain Jane you've been screwing the last few months?" asked Blackbeard. Jimmy clenched his teeth to the reference of Lorraine being a plain Jane and tried to conceal it. No one appeared to notice.

Two-step did not answer directly saying, "Let's just say my source has first-hand information that those safety deposit boxes have more money and valuables in them than the bank normally holds on a yearly basis. There are 150 boxes. Each of us will have close to 40 boxes to drill. The bank's going through cutbacks, and as of next Monday there'll no longer be an assistant manager--meaning that every time the alarm goes off, the same son-of-a-bitch manager has to respond--no more shared duties. The bank will close at 3:00 on Friday, Christmas Eve. We'll have that evening, Christmas Day, and the weekend to take care of business. The bank manager's an alcoholic, so we'll give him a few hours to visit his favorite bar, get a buzz-on, and start his drive home to his wife and kids, and then we set-off the alarm again. The cops are already getting pissed about responding to the bank's false alarms, and I've noticed they're slower to respond. Plus, when they do, they just hit the bank with lights, drive around the perimeter and leave--not waiting for the manager. Lately when he arrives, he only drives around the building, and he has only twice checked the doors We'll be inside the vault, so unless he changes his routine, we can finish the drilling, gather the goods, and be on our merry way Even if he enters the bank, he can't open the vault since it takes two individual codes. He shouldn't be able to smell any explosive residue with the type we're using.

"And, as Tiny Tim said, God bless everyone!" Jimmy shouted.

CHAPTER ONE

Jeannie was gasping for air as the aerobics instructor continued to shout commands: "Faster, faster, you can do it ladies." "How in the hell did I get in such bad shape?" she asked herself. "Well, dumb shit, you ate fast-food, never exercised, and drank until you blacked out, awakening with an unknow sex partner. What do you expect?" she thought. "Oh, and let's not forgot that you got yourself pregnant!"

It was ten days before Christmas Eve and Jeannie did not have a Christmas tree nor any Christmas decorations in her home. Fighting bouts of melancholy this time of the year, missing her mom and dad, she planned to go all-out this year, decorating not only the inside of her home, but the outside as well. She teared-up while thinking about those nights with her dad as a young child, helping him put up plywood cutouts of Santa and his sleigh on the front lawn. She remembered how he hung Christmas lights on the roof eves, and cursed and swore when they would not work. At that time, one burned-out bulb caused the entire strand to fail. So, there he would be in the cold with Jeannie, taking each and every bulb out and testing it. But, just like old Clark Griswold in the 1998 film, *Christmas Vacation*, her dad beamed with joy when their house was the brightest on the block.

At least her gym was decorated for the big day with Christmas ornaments hanging from the ceiling and garlands stretched across the walls. They even had small Christmas trees and poinsettia plants placed strategically at each row of exercise equipment, and a platter of sugar cookies and coffee by the front desk.

Jeannie had already decided the woman barking out commands was either former military, maybe a female Marine, or just an ego-driven lesbian getting thrills out of kicking a bunch of female asses. She always seemed to focus on the most attractive female "victims," and Jeannie was one of them. Wearing a white baseball hat with no wording or mascot on the front panel, and sporting a ponytail like almost all of the other women exercising, Jeannie wanted to strangle the exercise leader with every screamed command.

After her "self-confession" and "cleansing," the gym torture ended with Jeannie toweling herself off. She dialed the combination of her gym locker and grabbed her heavy backpack carrying her FBI badge Sig Sauer P226 9-millimeter. She walked to her new 2019 Corvette in the parking lot. After the near-death experience of being shot at the FBI satellite office and the resultant loss of her unborn baby, Jeannie decided that not only was it time to clean-up her life style, but also to have some fun instead of saving every penny of money she earned--a lesson taught by her parents. The torch-red Vette which she ordered fully loaded, looked fast just sitting in lot where she had purposely parked it away from other vehicles to prevent dings. Sure, it was impractical, but she loved the way the sportscar gripped the road at high speeds.

She climbed into the car's cockpit and took the cellphone from her bag, finding two missed calls. One was from Ismail Flores, one of her senior agents, and the other was yet another courtesy call from PG&E announcing a planned area power outage due to a transformer changeover--or something to that effect. She called Flores back, and without providing the usual greeting when he answered, she asked, "Are we set for the briefing at 2200 hours?"

"Merry Christmas to you too, Scrooge, and yes, we are. The bank surveillance team said the bad guys aren't there yet, so they're sticking to their normal schedule. We'll be notified once they show up. The rest of the team and SWAT will be here waiting for final instructions. You sound out of breath. Where are you? Not at a bar I hope."

"Sorry. Merry Christmas to you also--and no, as I told you, this is the new me. No more fast-food and booze, and plenty of exercise. Give me some credit, huh? It's been over six-months and I feel great."

"Just hassling you. Good job! The wifey and I want to have you over for a good, healthy, homecooked dinner once we wrap-up this case. You up for that?"

"Yes. I can put up with your shit as long as your beautiful wife is there. I love her. How are the kids? God, they must be getting old."

"Yeah, I don't know how that works. My wife and kids are getting older, but I'm still Chippendales material," Flores said while trying to suppress a laugh.

"Oh God! You're terrible. See you at 2200 hours," Jeannie said as she disconnected.

Jeannie had worked with Flores for several years, including the shootout with anarchists at the Roseville field office. Forty-years old and in good shape, Flores displayed male pattern baldness and a mustache which extended a half-inch down from his lower lip. He called it his "Poncho Villa stach," but Jeannie frequently corrected him saying, "Poncho Villa was a Mexican; you are Portuguese." When she took the assistant SAC job, she requested that Ismail Flores follow her there.

She deleted Flores's prior call and the one from PG&E; she was getting a little tired of the courtesy calls from her energy provider. For years PG&E never trimmed trees intertwined with their high-power lines. But now, after suffering a crippling financial loss following the November 8, 2018 fire that broke out in the early morning hours just outside Paradise, CA, home to many retirees, and faced with a bankruptcy filing, they started cutting-off power on windy days in the summertime. Now they were planning cut power in order to replace old equipment. "Guess this is the new normal," she thought.

PG&E's courtesy calls were to let everyone know that their power might be shut off, depending on their location. Talking to herself, she said, "Gee, thanks for the warning, assholes. Why haven't you guys done your job for the last 40-plus years? Oregon, Washington state, and even the Ukraine for God's sake trim the trees near their power lines; but no, not here in the highest taxed state. And now, after cutting power during the summer months, you want to screw with us going into the holidays, you clowns." The inferno consumed 20,000 acres and over 15,000 structures in one day; it also caused the deaths of at least 85 people Jeannie remembered. "Just covering their asses. That's all these annoying calls were," she said to herself. Jeannie arrived home and parked her Vette in the garage.

Jeannie usually drove a bureau car to work, crossing the Dumbarton Bridge from her home in Newark to Golden Gate Avenue in San Francisco where she worked as the Assistant SAC for the FBI. She and most of the special agents employed by the bureau could not afford rent in the city, much less own a home there; so, most opted to find residences in either the south or east bay regions, which still wasn't cheap compared to homes in the other forty-nine states.

Following the shootout at her previous post, a satellite bureau office located in Roseville, CA, Jeannie was offered the SAC position in San Francisco. She was told that there was going to be a purge of the liberal Obama appointees in the bureau and that they wanted her to be part of the replacement. Many of the "old regime" were facing serious crimes for their part in the 2016 presidential election, and the fallout was only beginning. Many on the "right" called it the Deep State, and from the rumors she heard, if only a small fraction of the rumors were true it would be the worst coup attempt in the history of the United States--getting FISA warrants on knowingly false information, bugging phones lines in the White House, staffing spies from Obama's former administration to bring down a duly-elected president. It was like a third-country coup.

Even though she felt more aligned to tenets of the Republican party, Jeannie was a registered Independent, telling anyone who inquired that she would always vote for the most suitable candidate, regardless of their political party. With the Presidential election coming soon in 2020, Jeannie already knew who she would be voting for since the Democratic challengers were all left-leaning crazies, as she described them. "God help the bureau and the country if any of those candidates somehow get in," she thought.

Jeannie informed her superiors that she was flattered to be offered the promotion to SAC, but requested that the appointment be to Assistant SAC--she could grow into the top position after gaining more experience. Personally, she hated San Francisco and what a third-world city it had become. When she was a kid, she always looked forward to visiting the "City-by-the-Bay," but that was before the Democrats took over the city bureaucracy and implemented their socialistic liberal ideas.

As a young girl she loved visiting Golden Gate Park: 1,017 acres of gardens, playgrounds, lakes, picnic groves, trails, and monuments. She was fascinated with the California Academy of Sciences, the de Young Museum, the Planetarium, the aquarium, the zoo, and especially a tour of Alcatraz prison. Her mom would pack a picnic lunch, and they would sprawl out on the lawn near the zoo and eat home-made potato salad and fried chicken.

Today there is a good chance of getting stuck with a throw-away hypodermic needle discarded by an addict who is sleeping, urinating and defecating in the park. A tourist hoping to enjoy a fun day at Pier 39 is likely to be hassled by a panhandler threatening an assault if felling blown-off, not to mention the chance of stepping into human waste on the sidewalk.

No, Jeannie hoped to stick-it-out at the San Francisco bureau office until she had enough experience to request a transfer to someplace near

Coeur d'Alene, Idaho. After her investigation of Frank Silva, Dr. Nancy Bell, and the Banshees in the infamous Ark of the Covenant case, she visited Silva's cabin overlooking Lake Coeur d'Alene. It was there that Jeannie believed Frank and Nancy devised their plan to steal the Ark of the Covenant from the small Chapel in Ethiopia. Jeannie contacted a local realtor and asked her to be on the alert for a place in the area becoming listed, and to let her know if one did. A few months later Jeannie toured a large, spacious log cabin and purchased the property as a vacation retreat. Whenever she could get away, she flew or drove to the cabin and relaxed, breathing in the mountain air and thinking about what happened to Silva and Dr. Bell.

Jeannie was able to convince her supervisors that taking the Assistant position was best for the bureau. She was also able to negotiate a transfer of her top agent, Ismail Flores, who like Jeannie hated San Francisco, but he wanted to continue working under Jeannie and was agreeable to making the change.

As Jeannie turn on the TV, she heard more PG&E warnings about wind gusts possibly reaching 70 mph in some areas of Northern California, quickly noting a web page she could use to determine if her area was going to be impacted with a power outage. "Wind event" was the new name coined for these incidents. These were not short-term power outages. They could be relatively short of up to 24-hours, or up to God knows how long. She heard from one of the other agents that PG&E needed to shut-down power lines several hours prior to a wind storm so the lines could cool.

She grabbed her Mac, and after typing in her address she read that her home was not slated for a planned power outage. Relieved to learn that she might not lose frozen food in her freezer, she began making herself a sandwich while continuing to monitor the news from the front room. Earlier, she had stopped at a Subway sandwich shop and bought a foot-long hot-roast-beef on a wheat roll. Not able to finish it, she brought it home and would now doctor it up for an early dinner.

From the TV she heard, "The Vatican announced today that Pope Francis will be visiting San Francisco in early March, 2020 to host a meeting with United States cardinals and other high-ranking church members, and to attend a conference at the Russian Orthodox cathedral to discuss the schism between the two Christian churches."

"Oh, that'll be great!" Jeannie said out loud. "Let's bring in that socialist pontiff who advocates open borders and let him see first-hand how a once beautiful city has turned into a third world dump with druggies camping on the street--and where almost every street reeks of human waste, not to mention the presence of used hypodermic needles everywhere. Ugh!"

Jeannie tried to attend mass regularly, opting for Saturday evening mass so she could sleep-in on Sunday mornings. She tried to shut her mind off when church dogma went against her political leanings, actually leaving on a few occasions when a particular deacon began telling the parishioners attending mass that the United States needs to open its borders to its "brothers and sisters."

"Fat chance," she thought. "Why don't you be the first, asshole? I'll bet your teenage daughters would have no problem with that. In fact, why don't you tell 'his holiness' that since he wants open borders, to tear down the Vatican walls!'

CHAPTER TWO

Jeannie took a cat-nap in anticipation of the night's event. She got off her bed and looked at herself in the mirror, noting that she needed to shampoo her hair even though she would be fixing it in a ponytail. She took off her San Francisco Giants baseball shirt and looked at her body. "Boobs still look good and my ass is still firm. Not bad for a 46-year-old," she thought. Her shoulder-length blond hair, hazel eyes and flirtatious smile sometimes got her into trouble. Friends and collogues described her as a look-a-like for either Gail O'Grady or Laura Vandervoort. She was happy with either comparison. The bullet wound scar near her belly button would be a conversation piece if and when she became intimate in the future, but there was no one of interest at the time.

Jeannie put on a bathrobe and walked out into her backyard. The sky was clear, and no fog was expected on her side of the bay; that probably would not be the case in the city. The fog generally rolls in around

5 p.m. and can get extremely thick as the night wears on. She hoped that would give her team some extra cover after nightfall.

She recalled her October interview with Lorraine Berkman, a Bank of America teller, after the bureau received a phone call from her stating that she had information about a planned bank robbery. Initially a male agent was scheduled to meet with Berkman and take her statement, and then to check the validity of her information. She said she would be embarrassed to speak with him and requested a female instead. Jeannie was the only one available and agreed to meet with her. During the interview she quickly realized that the Proverb--*"Hell hath no fury like a woman scorned"*--was right-on in this case.

Berkman was in her late sixties, but her hairstyle, makeup, and clothing made her appear much older. That she was slightly obese did not help. Some men, however, might see her as passable. Jeannie shook Berkman's hand after identifying herself and asked if she could get her anything, suggesting water, coffee or tea. Berkman asked if it was possible to get a diet Coke. Jeannie left and returned with a can of diet Coke, wondering to herself if this was part of Berkman's diet routine: eat anything, but wash it down with a diet soft drink.

"OK, Lorraine. You called saying you have information about a pending bank robbery. Is that correct?" Jeannie asked as she put the can of soda on the table.

"That's correct. I'm so stupid," she replied, and then started to cry. Reaching into her purse she first pulled out a Kleenex and then a folded piece of paper. "I guess I should start at the beginning, right?

"That might be best," Jeannie replied.

"As I said on the phone, I'm a bank teller with Bank of America, and I have been for fourteen years. The thought of taking a penny from the bank never crossed my mind. As you can see, I'm not a head-turner like you." Jeannie blushed, but did not speak. "I rarely socialize and when I do, it's with my church group. I normally stay home and take care of my mom who has pre-Alzheimer's. Well anyway, one night several months ago, it was either August or September, our church group hosted a small gathering in which we watched *Mary Poppins* together followed by cake and coffee. That's where I met Ronnie. He'd been invited to a small get-together by our pastor after saying that he recently moved into the area and was looking for a community church." She paused and took a swallow of soda. "He was temporarily living in a cheap motel until he found a house he could afford. Ronnie was pretty handsome and in good shape for a man his age. I learned he was 69-years old. I think there were about forty of us females at the get-together, and thinking back I should have seen what was coming." She started to cry a little harder. Jeannie felt she could ask a few questions at this juncture to allow Berkman a chance to regain her composure.

“Can I call you Lorraine?” Jeannie asked.

“Please do,” Berkman responded.

“First, do you know Ronnie’s last name?” Jeannie asked?

“He told me his last name was Roberts, but that was probably a lie,” Berkman said.

“So, you didn’t know him until he showed up at the church event. Is that correct?”

Berkman wiped her nose and dried her eyes while nodding her head up and down.

“OK, what did you mean when you said you should’ve seen what was coming?”

“You see, there were a lot of women there that night, and we outnumbered the guys 5:1. Most of the other females are a lot better looking than I am; and frankly, some of them dress like whores--showing black bra straps and wearing clothes that’re very revealing.”

“Shit!” Jeannie thought, “I’m wearing a black bra and matching panties right now. Glad I have a pullover sweater so my bra straps don’t show.”

“Go on,” Jeannie said.

“Well, Ronnie came up to me before the movie started and was really friendly. He said he had just moved here from Florida—that he’d gotten tired of the humidity. We laughed, we talked, we ate together.” She started to cry again. “You probably don’t understand since you’re used to getting a lot of attention because of how you look; but for me, to get all of Ronnie's attention even with some of those sluts throwing themselves at him--he wanted me. Well Ronnie and I started dating, you know, going out to dinner, church, picnics. He was a gentleman and never did anything inappropriate to me sexually. Finally, one day, Ronnie told me he was falling in love with me and that he wanted me to marry him. My God! My prayers had been answered."

Before she began speaking again, she took another gulp of soda and looked at Jeannie, then quickly glanced away. She said she and Ronnie started having sex. "He treated me as his princess. He would invite me to his apartment since we didn't want to make a scene in front of my mother. He'd have dinner waiting for me when I got home from the bank. He was always curious about my job." Jeannie noticed a rage beginning to build in Berkman's demeanor.

"Looking back at our conversations, I now see that he was sly about how he got information from me. You know--the names of my co-workers, how many supervisors we had, and was is it true that we actually have money that sprays dye on bank robbers? I now realize that I told him no one person has the total combination to the vault. I even told him about a recent birthday party we held in the bank for a co-worker, and now looking back, he was especially interested when I told him we had to put mylar balloons in one room at the close of the business day because our motion detectors are so sensitive, they'll pick-up the balloons' movement when the heater comes on. I actually told him that the bank really doesn't keep a lot of money on site--that the real value was in our customer's safety deposit boxes. Can you believe how stupid I was?" she asked Jeannie.

Jeannie did not speak, hoping that Berkman would not pick up on her agreement and would go on. "After a while, Ronnie started to change. He was always busy with projects and we started spending less and less time together. I thought it was my fault. I tried to talk with him about the upcoming holidays and what his traditions were. I was in love with him.

One day, I decided to surprise him with a little treat when he got home." Her face got redder than a polished Washington State apple. "I had gone shopping at Victoria Secret and got a sexy black lingerie set. Black was Ronnie's favorite color. I planned on cooking him dinner, and then after retreating to the bathroom surprise him with my outfit. By this time, the motel manager knew me, and seeing my hands full of purchases, let me into Ronnie's room." She took out a folded piece of notepaper and passed it to Jeannie. "Here's the address to his motel." Jeannie looked at it. From the address she knew that Ronnie did not live in the high-rent district.

"While I was waiting for his return, I went into the bedroom envisioning how I wanted my entrance to be later that evening. The phone on the nightstand rang, and as I picked it up, I smacked my toe on the table leg and dropped it without saying hello. I got down on my knees to get the phone and saw a bunch of drawings under the bed. I'm ashamed that I pulled them out and looked at them, but it was because of what I saw that I'm here today."

"While you were dating him, did you ever meet any of his friends or associates?" Jeannie asked.

"Only one. Ronnie and I went out to dinner together one night. Actually, it was a KFC place and we decided to just eat there. We were sitting there eating and this really thin guy comes up to our table and says 'Hi' to Ronnie. He didn't call Ronnie by name, he just tapped him on the shoulder and asked, 'What's up?' I think his name was Jimmy, but I'm not sure. Anyway, he gave me the creeps. He stared at my breasts and made me feel awkward. Ronnie wasn't happy to see him and just gave him a high-fist. He pointed to me and gave the guy my name and went back to his meal. I said 'Hi,' but the guy just stood there staring at me. I guess he got the hint that Ronnie was not in a talkative mood and went to the counter and placed an order. Once he got his food, he turned to our table, but he didn't say anything--just more stares. I never saw the guy again."

After about 90-minutes of interview, Jeannie thanked Lorraine for the information, gave her a business card, and told her to call if she thought of anything else. Lorraine said she would. Then standing, she shook Jeannie's hand and left.

Burkman took one of the elevators down to the main floor and left the building, not noticing that across the street in a parked silver Ford Focus was the same man who gave her the creeps in KFC. He had been following her since seeing her leave with Two-step from KFC a few weeks before. Why was Lorraine visiting the Federal Building, he wondered? Was she there because of income tax problems or did she get stuck with a juror summons? Should he tell Two-step? He thought, "Fuck him. The way he treated me that night at the chicken place!"

CHAPTER THREE

The information Jeannie obtained from Lorraine Berkman was based solely on a drawing of the bank location and what appeared to be a line drawn from Van Ness Avenue to the bank. The dates, December 24-26, were circled. Lorraine did not have time to examine the drawings thoroughly; she heard a key being inserted into the door and quickly placed them back under the bed. Ronnie was surprised to see her in his apartment, but acted lovey-dovey. Berkman, sensing Ronnie's excitement to see her, quickly rationalized that what she had seen was nothing and did not bring it up as a topic of conservation.

Jeannie knew there was not enough evidence to obtain a search warrant, and if in fact this Ronnie dude was planning a heist, on what day or time would he or they hit? But Jeannie suspected that Berkman's female intuition was correct. Ronnie, or whatever his true identity was, got the information he was seeking, maybe a little sex as well, and dropped her as soon as he could.

Jeannie met with Flores after Berkman left the bureau and told him what Berkman had said. "A little thin don't you think?" he asked.

"Yes, and even if we found a prosecution-friendly judge to issue a warrant, even a mediocre defense attorney would shred it in discovery," Jeannie replied. "I ran Ronald Roberts through the system with as much information as I could from what Berkman told me, but I came up with nothing. She's probably right--a false name."

"What do you want to do?" Flores asked.

"Well, we could start a surveillance on Ronnie and his room, and see if we can identify him and any associates. Maybe even contact the manager and try to sweet-talk our way into his apartment and see what we can find."

"Yeah, but we run the risk of being seen; or worse, what if that damn apartment manager is in on the robbery--you know, part of the gang," Flores said waiting for a reply as Jeannie tapped her desk with a pen in deep thought.

"We could always go off-the-books," she finally said.

"Wow, just promoted to the Assistant SAC and she wants to play a female James Bond. I'm in. Got nothing else to do except worry about my pregnant wife getting bigger on Thanksgiving."

"You know, you can be an asshole at times. Your wife is the love of your life and you know it. So what if she puts on a few extra pounds. It's Thanksgiving. She's been pretty good about watching her weight up until now. Besides, mister, I think a lot of that Portuguese linguica you've been eating lately has shifted south, or haven't you noticed?" Jeannie asked.

"Hey, more for her to love," he replied. "So, when do you want to go James Bonding?"

"Berkman said that Ronnie normally meets with friends on Thursday nights. These may be confederates, but instead of putting a team on him, you and I can watch his apartment starting at 5 p.m. When we see him leave, we check out his place. If we find anything interesting, we can decide what to do next."

"Sexy and cunning. God, I have a great boss," Flores said while trying not to laugh.

"Hey, you know you don't have to do this with me tonight. If we're caught, losing our jobs will be the least of it," Jeannie said.

"I know you remember when we worked that Star Chamber case– the one where that secret court tried people in absentia and if found guilty, carried out death sentences?" Flores asked.

"You mean the case where I ended up shot? Gee, I think I remember. What's your point? I'm just trying to give you an out." Jeannie responded.

"No, no, I know. I just wanted to say that somewhere inside me I thought that the Star Chamber concept was correct. Those people they killed had it coming. They all thought they were above the law because of their fame and fortune. You know, like when those Death Wish movies with Charles Bronson came out, and almost everyone in the movie and in the audience cheered at his vigilante antics. And, how most law enforcement types would love to do some of the things that Dirty Harry did." Flores stopped, watching for a reaction from Jeannie who remained speechless for a few seconds but then said, "So, you want to be Dirty Flores and clean up San Francisco?"

"Yes. Can't you see me saying in my Portuguese accent, '*Go ahead, make my day*.'"

While Jeannie tried to contain her laugh, Flores said, "I'm just saying that the law today seems to be overwhelmingly on the side of suspects. The victims get forgotten. You know what I'm trying to say. Sometimes a good law enforcement officer has to operate off the books, and if the ends justify the means, so be it. That's all I'm saying. So, with that said, I'll see you here at what? 4:00 p.m.?"

"No, I'll come to your house and pick you up. We'll use the Vette so if we're seen, no one will suspect we're the Feds."

"Gee, can I drive? You know, it is almost Christmas," he said laughing.

Two-step was again the first member of the group to enter the bar. As soon as the others showed-up, he got the attention of the bartender and ordered two pitchers of dark beer and a pizza. As soon as the pitchers of beer, mugs, and pizza arrived they all dug-in, making small-talk while eating. With the pizza consumed and beer mugs refilled, Two-step retrieved an 8 ½ by 12-inch binder sitting beside him and put it on the table. Before opening it, he said, "Tonight I'll pick each of you up around 10:00 p.m. Be ready. I'll have already set off the alarm with the pulse gun from across the street two times, starting at 1:00 p.m. since the bank closes at three. The last time the bank manager arrived, he cruised around the perimeter and left. The cops did the same thing. I'll set it off again just before we enter the tunnel. Blackbeard, you'll bring in the explosives and lights. Apache, you'll carry in the large tarp. Jimmy, you carry in the drills.

The shape charge shouldn't activate the alarm; but even if it does, the manager and cops will be so pissed-off with it being Christmas Eve and Christmas Day that I doubt anyone will exit their vehicles. And even if they do decide to look into the bank from the outside, they'll see nothing out of the ordinary. We'll have all Christmas Day to hit the safety deposit boxes, but let's get in and out as quickly as possible. Any questions?"

CHAPTER FOUR

AFGHANISTAN MOUNTAINS

"Saif, Abu, Khalid. Come, come, sit down," said Ayman Baghdadi sitting with his back against the cave wall, an AK-47 next to his side. Baghdadi had taken over leadership of Al-Qaeda after several others had fallen at the hands of American drone attacks and assassinations.

"I hope you had a good journey," he said. The three bearded men nodded yes. They ranged in ages from 25 to 32 years, and all three had traveled from Libya fully knowing the nature of their meeting with Baghdadi.

"Allah has chosen you three to bring the great Satin to its knees as envisioned by Osama bin Laden before his execution by the Americans. Our organization founded by our fallen leader has been silent for too long. During our silence, ISSI and other groups have been the focus of America, and we have spent most of our energy trying to reorganize. With your actions, the Americans will learn that al Qaeda is strong and can strike again on their homeland.

Although other brothers and sisters already in America will create acts of jihad, their actions will only be distractions, allowing you to carry out bin Laden and Allah's true purpose." Baghdadi motioned to an older male who entered the cave carrying fruits on a tray and asked where to put the food items. "Eat my brothers and I will explain your task."

As each of the three took items from the tray, Baghdadi studied them closely. The same man who delivered the fruit platter returned carrying three backpacks and handing one to each visitor. "Inside your packs, you will find airline tickets, passports and visas. You do not have to worry about security since we learned from 9-11 what American security now looks for to identify terrorists. Your tickets were purchased on different dates using a clean Visa or Mastercard, and you will be spaced out on the plane in coach, not first class. You will check-in luggage like a normal tourist would do for a long flight. The Americans will be looking for people paying for tickets with money and not carrying any luggage--something your brothers did on that great day when they destroyed symbols of American greed and killed thousands of infidels.

For your mission you are granted by Allah to shave your beards upon arrival." The three looked at each other unsure how to respond. They remained silent. Baghdadi continued, "When you arrive in San Francisco, you will each take a separate taxi to a hotel listed in your backpack. This will be the first time you will be together during your trip. You each have a credit card in your name in the pack. You will research different locations for the purchase of your scuba equipment and purchase them on separate dates while traveling alone. The burner phones in your packs are to be used only in an emergency. Keep them turned on once you arrive so we can notify you when and where to meet to receive the rest of your equipment. The explosives will take longer to smuggle into the United States. While you are doing this, you will start hearing about actions taken by your brothers and sisters. Do not be concerned about them. This is what the Americans call a smokescreen which will draw their resources away from you should they somehow start to suspect something. Come closer please so I can show you your target. You recognize San Francisco, yes?"

CHAPTER FIVE

Jeannie arrived at Flore's residence at 4:30 p.m. wanting to visit for a short time with his wife. Seven months pregnant, Flore's wife gave a warm hug when Jeannie entered the home. "Jeannie, it's been too long. How are you? You look great," she said.

The Flore's home smelled great, and Jeannie could only guess that the aromas emanated from mint, allspice, cinnamon and other Portuguese spices. She could also smell something being deep fried and guessed that it had to be her favorite: Portuguese donuts. Jeannie overdramatized taking in a deep breath and asked, "Is that what I think it is?"

Flores's wife had a huge grin on her face and said, "Yes, malasadas, just for you."

Ismail entered the kitchen and seeing Jeannie asked, "Did you bring my car?"

Flore's wife ignored him as did Jeannie who watched as freshly cooked malasadas where being pulled from a deep fryer and placed on a rack so excess oil could drain off and cool. Shortly, Flore's wife placed a few donuts into a brown paper bag Jeannie knew had sugar and cinnamon inside. She shook the bag and the malasadas were removed and placed on a decorative plate in front of where Jeannie was sitting.

Flores said, "I'm ready. I guess we should get going."

His wife glared at him but said nothing. Neither did Jeannie who watched as a cup of coffee was poured for her by Ismail's wife. Jeannie grabbed a donut and took a bite. "Oh man, these are so great!"

"Thank you," said Flore's wife, with a big smile.

"Oh hell, I might as well have a few myself," Ismail said as he reached for a malasada.

"What about your diet?" his wife asked.

"More for you to love my darling," Ismail responded, giving her a kiss in the process.

"Oh, how cute," said Jeannie, looking at Ismail.

They said goodbye to Flore's wife and started walking to Jeannie's car. "Here, just keep the four tires on the ground, huh," said Jeannie as she tossed him the keys to the Vette. Flores caught the keys and hit the remote key access. "Hey, would it be OK if I drive around the block of my old girlfriend's house and honk the horn a few times so she'll look out the window? You won't have to slide down in your seat since I want her to see me driving my red Corvette with a blonde sitting next to me."

"Sounds OK with me, but let's check with your wife first," Jeannie said laughing. "Alright, let's get serious."

She pushed the Vette's GPS showing directions to the apartment. "When we get close, find a place to park so we can watch the place and see if he's home. If we don't see any movement, I'll go up to the door and knock. If he answers, I'll act shocked as if I got the wrong apartment number. If there's no answer, I'll pick the lock, and when you see me enter, come and join me. Sound OK with you?" Jeannie asked.

"Yeah, but what do we do it he walks in on us?" Flores asked.

"I don't know. You're the Die-Hard guy. Maybe you could just shoot him," Jeannie said smiling.

"Boy, you're on a roll today, aren't you?" Ismail responded. "What did you do? Get laid before you came and picked me up?"

"I told you, those days are behind me. Maybe I'll find my prince someday, but right now I have to continue cleaning-up my act and concentrating on my job. If you must know, I actually went to church this afternoon," she said.

"Church! You mean the roof didn't collapse, the holy water didn't boil, and the place didn't burst into flames when you entered?" he asked.

"What does your wife see in you?" she asked, trying unsuccessfully to suppress a laugh.

"Hey, you've never had a Portuguese lover. Once you have a Portagee, you can't be satisfied with anyone else." He chuckled and continued, "You know what they say about Latin lovers. So why did you go to church on a Saturday?"

"St. Edwards has a Saturday night mass that starts at 5 p.m., and I decided that I'd start going back to church. I've been thinking a lot about my dad. It always happens this time of the year. You know: Halloween, Thanksgiving, Christmas. Anyway, when I was still married to you-know-who, we got a call one night from my mom that my grandfather was in the hospital and it was bad. He had a bad heart you know."

"Yeah, you told me about him. How old was he then?"

"Gee, I guess he was in his mid-eighties at the time," Jeannie said.

"Anyway, we drove to the hospital and when we got there, he'd been placed in an isolation ward since they weren't sure what was wrong. Tests came back showing he had a bad heart valve that was causing fluid to build up in his lungs. When we entered his room, two people only, he said 'Hi' to us, but then after a short time, he asked if he could speak with me privately. As soon as you-know-who left, he reached out to grab my hand, and asked me to promise that I would take care of my grandmother when he was gone." Jeannie caught herself choking-up and paused, looking out the window of her sportscar.

"I tried to joke with him and told him he wasn't going anywhere, but he squeezed my hand and asked me to promise, which I did. Then, without releasing my hand, he asked me why I wasn't going to church anymore? I didn't hesitate and told him that with all the death and hate I see in my work, I started doubting there was a God."

"Oh, I bet that went over well," said Ismail as he slowed for a stop light. "Well, what did he say?"

"He released my hand and I thought that was it, but instead he told me a story I hadn't heard before. My grandfather was in the Navy, enlisting right after the Japanese bombed Pearl Harbor. After pushing the Japanese back to their home islands, his ship arrived off the coast of Saipan. From the position of his ship, he was shocked at watching Japanese mothers throw their children, many just babies, off cliffs into the sea before they, too, dove to their deaths. So many chose suicide rather than be in the hands of Americans, that their and their children's bodies banged into the side of both his and other allied ships around the island.

As shocked as his fellow shipmates by the dead bodies around their ship, he talked to the ship's Chaplin--asking how God could allow something like this to happen?"

"You know, I'm a Catholic and I have had those thoughts myself," said Ismail. "What did the Chaplin tell your grandfather?" he asked.

"The Chaplin basically said we are not able to understand why God allows bad things to happen. He explained it by asking my grandfather a question:

'Is it not true that if everyone followed the 10 commandments, nothing would ever be stolen, no spouse would be betrayed, no one's son or daughter would be murdered?' Of course, my grandfather said 'no,'" Jeannie said. "Rather than control us, the Chaplin said, God gives us freedom. God does not interfere with anyone's choices. Rather he assures us that everyone will someday answer for what they have done, and that justice will be administered. Judgment will be based on the guidelines given. The problem is, being told how to live well, is insufficient.

He told my grandfather that his question asking how God could allow bad things like what he just witnessed off the coast of Saipan as the most commonly asked questions in life. But more often than not, we don't get a straightforward answer to this seemingly simple question, and not getting all the answers can definitely test our faith. When bad things happen, we might sometimes wonder where God is. If He's really there. If He could have prevented it. If He could have sent a miracle.

Unfortunately, we might not always know the reason 'why' bad things happen, and I can't tell you with any certainty why God allows them to take place. But we can always draw faith and strength from remembering the things we *do* know. The Chaplin ended his talk with my grandpa by saying that even though God doesn't cause evil, he permits it. And as a Chaplin, he said, I know that if God permits something, he plans to bring a greater good out of it. All that you and I can do is trust." Jeannie stopped and waited for a response from Ismail. Several seconds passed with silence consuming the interior of the Corvette.

"So, after your grandfather told you this story, you felt compelled to go to church this afternoon, huh?" he finally said.

"Yes, from that day on, he put the Catholic guilt trip on me and I have tried to go to mass each week," Jeannie replied. "And this evening, something weird happened to me."

"Pray tell," Ismail said, enjoying shifting through the gears after stopping for a red light.

"Well, I haven't gone to confession in a long, long time."

"Hell girl, you could tell me your confession anytime you want. I bet it would be hot. No?" Ismail asked while laughing.

"Shut up. Do you want to know what happened or not? By the way, we are only a few miles away," she said.

"Yeah, yeah, go on, but don't leave out the juicy parts, OK?" said Ismail.

"You're a pervert," interjected Jeanie, and continued. "When I got there, I was the only one. I chose, as I normally do, to sit near the back of the church. The priest came in from the front and walked down the main aisle, nodding at me as he passed.

He entered the confessional box and two green lights came on, indicating that a person could come in and confess.

"You jumped up and could hardly wait to go in there and make the priest's day confessing your previous extracurricular sexual and drinking activities. Boy, I bet the holy water was boiling," Ismail jokingly said.

Jeannie hit his right arm hard, causing Ismail to say, "Ouch, you know it is a felony to hit a Federal agent? OK, go on."

"Well, a young girl, maybe six or seven entered the church from a side entrance near the front. A few seconds later a heavy-set male whom I assumed was her dad, entered--following her to a pew. After a short time, the little girl got up and walked into the confessional. She was only in there a few minutes, and then she came bouncing out, running to her dad. She told her dad in an audible voice that Father was waiting for him. He told his daughter that he still needed a few more minutes. She scampered off again and re-entered the confessional, again running back to her dad saying that the priest said it would be alright. Instead of getting up and going to the confessional, her father continued to kneel and pray.

A short time later, I heard a door to the confessional open and the priest came out and started walking towards the little girl's dad. You know me, I couldn't help myself from watching the event unfold. The priest talked almost in a whisper to the girl's father, while placing his hand on his shoulder. The man shook his head up and down and I heard him sobbing. The priest walked out of the pew and started walking back to the confessional; then, turned to me and said, "OK, your next; come with me."

"Oh shit! What did you do?" asked Ismail.

"Oh shit, is right! He waited for me to get up and follow him. My heart was beating fast and I had thoughts of making a quick left at the rear door, jumping into my car and getting the hell out of there; but something happened. Now, don't laugh or I'll have to shoot you. The strangest feeling came over me. I followed him into the confessional, which if you haven't gone for a while, is set up so you have a choice of kneeling behind a curtain or going face-to-face with the priest. I chose to sit across from him face-to-face. He looked at me and I started off with, you know, 'Bless me father for I have sin. It has been….' I had to stop, and I told him that it has been years since I confessed.

I waited for the chastisement, but he said jokingly, "Well, it is about time."

I felt compelled to tell him why I had stopped going to church in the past, and how the talk with my grandfather when he was in the hospital made me return. I told him I was divorced two times over and how I still had a lot of problems with some of the church's ideology dealing with politics. To my amazement he said, 'Ah, the Church doesn't know what direction to take. There are too many Cardinals and priests who have taken a liberal approach to our doctrine and I fear we are moving in the wrong direction.'

I got the impression that he, too, was upset with the current Pope and the socialistic attitude he seemed to bring to the papacy. Then, I started to cry and opened up about, you know, all the things I am not proud of, and how I am trying to change my life for the good. I really lost it when I talked about the Roseville field office incident. I told him I was an FBI agent. Once I got control of myself, I said I'm probably going to hell since I still receive Holy Communion without going to confession--feeling that it is between me and God and I don't need a priest as an intermediary. You know what he said?" Jeannie asked Ismail, who had not interrupted her while she was speaking.

"Ten-thousand Our Fathers, and five-thousand Hail Mary's?" he asked.

"Very funny. No, he said that ultimately it was between me and God and that if I truly love God and try to the best of my ability to live a good Christian life, who is he--a priest--to judge me. I felt a warmth came over me, and I couldn't remember how many Our Father's, or Hail Mary's I had to do as penance. I shook his hand and thanked him. When leaving he said to remember what Jesus said about 'blessed are the peacemakers' and to be safe. And since that happened, I have to admit that I've experienced more good things in my life than bad. OK, Jerk. Let me have it," Jeanne said turning away from Ismail, looking out the passenger window.

To her surprise, Ismail was silent for a long time as if to take it all in, especially since she had dominated the conversation after leaving his house. Finally, after clearing his throat, he said, "Wow! That is an amazing story."

"Go ahead Ass. I can take your sarcasm," Jeannie said.

"No, honestly, I don't know what to say," he responded. "I mean, you know, I'm Catholic too, but I've never had an experience like that in my life. I've heard similar stories, but it's never happened to me." The rest of the ride concluded in silence.

CHAPTER SIX

Jeannie walked up to the motel, checking her surroundings--especially the office area. A light drizzle was falling and there was an occasional gust of wind. Seeing no one in the area, she knocked on Ronnie's door. Her hair in a ponytail, she wore a black knit watch cap and black leather jacket--the look completed with knee-high black boots. She was wearing skin-colored plastic gloves. Maybe, if anyone was watching she could pass as a prostitute. Better not share that thought with Ismail. She would never hear the end of it, she thought.

Receiving no answer to her knock, she glanced over her shoulder while pulling out her lock picking kit. It had been her father's, a retired police officer. He taught her how to pick locks when the weather was not conducive to playing outside when she was young. They played games to see who could open the same lock the quickest. When she started to get good at it, her dad made her do it blindfolded in the dark.

"You don't want someone seeing you with a flashlight in your mouth working on someone's lock, do you?" he would say. She won several times, but looking back now since her dad had passed away, she was sure he allowed her to win. "No time to reminisce tonight Dad," Jeannie said to herself. "We need to get in and out without getting our asses caught."

The lock was not much of a challenge; it certainly was not a grade one deadbolt. In less than 20 seconds Jeannie conquered the lock and opened the door to Ronnie's room. Before closing the door, she took out her handheld Hatori mini-flashlight and aimed it across the street towards Ismail, flashed it one time. She then closed the door and made sure the cheap curtains in the room were fully pulled shut so no one from the outside could see the flashlight beam.

Ismail saw the light and got out of the car. He placed both of his gloved hands in the pockets of a ragged navy peacoat, rearranged his black San Francisco Giants baseball cap on his head, and walked slowly across the street to the apartment. Once there, he opened and then closed the door--relocking it.

"Gee, what a fuckin' dump. Smells like trash throw-out at a fast-food restaurant. Look at that mattress," he said after focusing his penlight on the bed. "I bet it could tell a few stories, huh?"

"Focus buddy, so we can get the hell out of here," Jeannie replied.

"Yeah, yeah. How do you want to do this?" Ismail asked.

"Well, it's not a big place and it looks like the Spartans decorated it. There is hardly anything here, and it looks like Ronnie doesn't stay here much. Do you want the bathroom or this room?" Jeannie asked.

"I'll take the bathroom and meet up with you shortly. Shouldn't take a whole lot of time," he replied.

Flores found an empty medicine cabinet in the bathroom. There was a wastepaper basket, but either it had not been used or someone had emptied it. Opening the toilet lid, he found standing urine. "Guess the motherfucker is too lazy to flush," he thought. "Waste of time in here," he called out to Jeannie while returning to her location. "Nothing of value in here except that," she said, pointing in the direction of another wastepaper basket containing an empty Chinese takeout carton and two partially-full paper drinking cups of soda. Oh, and I found a stash of his reading material. Looks like the stuff you read," pointing to porn magazines located on an end table to the right of the bed.

"Hey, he's a well-read man. What can I say?" Ismail said, thumbing through one of the magazines. "I didn't know you posed for Playboy back in the day," he said, showing her the centerfold page of the magazine. Jeannie hit him in the face with the beam of her high-intensity flashlight. "Well shit! Looks like we come-up empty," Ismail said, putting the magazines back on the end table in the same fashion he found them.

"Maybe not," said Jeannie as she walked over to the wastebasket near the TV.

"What do you suggest Sherlock?" Ismail asked, already knowing what she was thinking.

"OK, try this on. Somewhere down the line, if this leads anywhere, we're going to have to show how we got the true identification of Ronnie, right? That's if he's in any system." Not waiting for an answer, she went on. "So, we take the trash containing the pizza box with us, but more importantly, the soda cups."

"Yeah, I follow you. That's how they caught the Bay Area Rapist over in Sacramento a year or so ago. Got a cup out of his garbage can he'd put on the street. But what happens if this asshole comes home and sees that the garbage isn't here?" Ismail asked.

"Look at this place. Do you think Ronnie pays any notice to what this place looks like? He'll see the trash gone and think the maid service took it."

"OK. But again, so what? We process the cups for DNA and let's say we get a hit. 'How did you get the cups to begin with, Agent Loomis?' the defense attorney will ask."

"I've already thought about that. We write a report saying that we saw the maid go into his room and take out the wastepaper basket. We saw her place it in a large receptacle, and we immediately retrieved it. No expectation of privacy for common trash, therefore a legal search."

"God! Smart and pretty. That will work. Let's get the hell out of here then," said Ismail as he shut off his flashlight and started for the door with Jeannie following. "Do you want to head down to the bureau with the evidence or wait until tomorrow?" he asked.

"We both know we're still on a little shaky ground here regarding the search, so let's not compound it by saying that we locked the evidence in our car overnight," she replied. "Let's drop it off and make it all legal-like, and then I'll take you out for an early breakfast. Sound good?" she asked.

"Sounds good to me, Boss."

CHAPTER SEVEN

The drive across Dumbarton bridge seemed lighter than normal the following morning. Jeannie enjoyed lowering the passenger window a crack in her Corvette so she could smell the salt-water breeze as she progressed through the gears. She hoped that upon arrival this morning she would find results of the DNA tests she and Ismail requested. She parked the Vette in the underground secured garage and went through security at the rear of the building. Her thoughts drifted back to the FBI branch office assault in Roseville that resulted in the death of her supervisor as well as the bullet injury to her abdomen that caused her to lose her unborn baby. "I wish we had been provided the security in Roseville like the protection we have here," she thought.

Getting off the elevator on the top floor and walking towards her office she ran into Ismail who showed a thumbs-up, indicating they got a hit on both soda cups. "Seriously?" Jeannie asked.

"Yup, we got Ronnie identified," he replied.

"Good morning Jeannie," said Tami, the secretary she shared with the SAC. "Ismail told me. Congratulations!"

"Thanks, but we haven't got anything yet," Jeannie said as she asked Flores to follow her to the cafeteria for a coffee and sweet roll. During the walk she asked him about the returns from forensics.

"His real name is Daniel Payne, a sixty-nine-year-old white male. He did a five-year stretch for burglary in 1990, but got out after three and a half years due to good behavior. I just received that when I came in, so that's all I have. Maybe we can give what we have to Darcy and let her do a workup. What do you think?"

Darcy applied for the vacant computer forensic post at the San Francisco office, wanting to follow Jeannie and Ismail there since she too was involved in the Roseville office shootout. She was a paper-chaser and one of the best computer wizards the bureau had in tracking-down individuals trying to hide their criminal enterprises in off-shore accounts, shell companies, or the dark web.

"I think that's a good idea. Let's see if she's in. Rumor has it that she has no personal life, coming in early for work and leaving late. Maybe she can do a quick check on Payne while we wait. Remember the date Berkman saw on the drawing in 'Ronnie's' apartment--December 25, Christmas Day? That's coming up soon."

"Hi Jeannie; Hi Ismail. How are you two?" she asked, arising from her chair when they entered her computer lab.

"Hi Darcy. How do you like it here? A lot different than the small office you had in Roseville, right?" Jeannie asked.

"Oh, heck yes. Look at the space in here," she replied as Ismail walked around the room counting the number of computers and other equipment; he had no clue what they did. "What brings you to my humble abode?" she asked.

Ismail placed the DNA match information file on Darcy's desk. Jeannie told Darcy what they were investigating and expressed an urgency in knowing everything they could about Payne. She asked Darcy if she had time to run it down for them with Christmas only a few weeks away. Darcy said she would love to work with them again, especially on a case much more interesting than a hedge fund manager trying to hide assets. "Let's see what we can find right now," she said, typing information into her computer.

"Got something! Daniel Payne, sixty-nine years old, white male. He served time at Folsom Prison. Let's see, I found his DD214. He was in the U.S. Army for two years. Did one year in Vietnam," Darcy said while typing so fast that both Jeannie and Ismail lost track of what she was doing.

"How did you get his DD214?" Ismaeil asked.

"You really don't want to know," she replied. Jeannie looked at Ismail as if to say, "Stop interrupting her!" "Can you give me an hour to check some other possible sources? I can come up to your office when I get through."

"That would be great, anything you can get on him and any known associates--you know, the usual?" Jeannie said as she and Flores left Darcy's office.

***

United Airline flight 930 arrived in San Francisco from Algeria at 10:15 a.m. Three Algerian males grabbed their carry-on luggage from their respective overhead compartments, never establishing eye contact with one another. One male was wearing faded blue jeans, sandals, and a t-shirt with a soccer team logo. The other two wore black and red shirts, gray leather jackets, tan pants, and black slip-on shoes. All were clean-shaven.

They met-up with each other in the taxi-zone area, but took separate taxis to a motel in South San Francisco, arriving at slightly different times. Two took a room together, while the other had a room to himself. Exhausted from their trip and with knowledge of their mission, they turned in for the night. The next day they would receive instructions on how to proceed.

The flight from Morocco containing the second terrorist team arrived at the San Francisco

International Airport at 11:15 p.m. As the al Qaeda leader predicted, the three Libyans had no problem proceeding through security checkpoints, either leaving Morocco or at their point of entry in Washington. Now together, they could proceed according to plan.

The third jihadist team arrived at the San Francisco International Airport from New York one day after the first two teams. Of the three Algerians males, only Basem Tinazzi could speak English. He was also the youngest. Khalil Qasim and Sami Marek were brother-in-law's, and they had become jihadists after being indoctrinated by Basem.

They hailed a cab and with luggage in hand, requested the cabbie to take them to the Ritz-Carlton hotel. Only small talk took place between Basem and the driver of the cab. He told the driver that the three of them were reporters and were there to attend the upcoming presidential rally in the city. Upon arriving at the Ritz-Carlton, Basem asked the driver to wait a few minutes while he checked-out the inside of the hotel. Khalil and Sami remained in the taxi. When he returned, he told the driver to proceed to the Hampton Inn, in Daly City.

"That's going to be a big fare," the driver said before pulling out of the driveway.

"That is fine my friend. Please drive us there," Basem said as the other two just looked at him, having no idea what was being said.

CHAPTER EIGHT

At 11:15 a.m. Jeannie's office phone rang. It was Darcy asking if she could bring down information she found on Payne. When she arrived, Flores was already in the room, as were agents Tim Harrison and Nina Reilly. Darcy knocked on Jeannie's closed door. "Come in," Jeannie said.

"Hi Darcy, I think you know everyone, don't you?" she asked.

Darcy blushed and tried to hide her shyness while carrying a file in her left-hand. "Yes, hello everyone," she replied. Finding the only empty chair in the room, she sat next to Nina and placed the file she was carrying on her lap.

"I've already told Nina and Tim that 'Ronnie' is actually Daniel Payne, but that is about it. So, blow us away with what you found," said Jeannie.

Darcy opened the file and apologized for not having copies for everyone. Jeannie said to go on, and that she would arrange for copies to be made later.

Darcy said that Payne was drafted during the Vietnam conflict. He received his initial training at Fort Ord in Monterey county, California. After he got out of basic training, he was trained as a tunnel rat."

"What's a tunnel rat?" Nina asked.

Darcy explained: "Tunnel rats were American, Australian, and New Zealand soldiers who performed underground search and destroy missions during the Vietnam War. In the early stages of the war against the French colonial forces, the Viet Minh created an extensive underground system of tunnels which were later expanded and improved by the Viet Cong. By the 1960s, the tunnel complexes included hospitals, training areas, storage facilities, headquarters, and barracks. These tunnels were so sophisticated they had ventilation systems, allowing VC guerrillas to remain hidden underground for months at a time.

Tunnel rats were given the task of entering these tunnels and destroying them after gathering whatever intelligence was inside, killing or capturing their occupants—often in conditions of close combat. Typically, a tunnel rat was equipped with only a standard issued .22 pistol or M1917 revolver, a bayonet, a flashlight, and explosives. Tunnel rats were generally men of smaller stature--five-foot six and under--who were able to maneuver more comfortably in the narrow tunnels. Payne is five-foot seven."

"I had a next-door neighbor who was a tunnel rat. He died about three years ago. The stories he told me after a few beers raised the hairs on my arms. Besides enemy combatants, the tunnels themselves presented many potential dangers to tunnel rats. Sometimes they were poorly constructed, and they would simply collapse. Tunnels were often booby trapped with hand grenades, anti-personnel mines, and punji sticks," Ismail said.

"What's a punji stick?" Nina again asked.

"It's a simple spike made out of wood or bamboo that has been sharpened and heated. The VC would then urinate or shit on the spikes to pass infection on to poor saps who stepped on them," Flores answered, and continued, "The VC would even use venomous snakes placed as living booby traps. Rats, spiders, scorpions, and ants all posed threats to tunnel rats. Bats also roosted in the tunnels, although they were generally more of a nuisance than a threat. Tunnel construction occasionally included anti-intruder features such as U-bends that could be flooded quickly to trap and drown tunnel rats. Sometimes poison gases were used. I tell you, tunnel rats had ice water in their veins. Sorry for the interruption, Darcy," turning the meeting back to her.

"Yes," said Darcy, and Payne was decorated for his actions as a tunnel rat while in the Cu Chi region of Vietnam--which had the most tunnels. His nickname was Two-step."

"Before anyone asks, 'Two-step' was a name given to a dangerous venomous snake that soldiers encountered in the jungle. The myth was that if you got bitten by this snake, you only got two-steps left of your life," Ismail said, now embarrassed for his interruptions.

Darcy continued, "He received an honorable discharge from the Army, declining an offer to re-enlist. A friend at the Pentagon did some digging for me and found that one of Payne's fellow tunnel rats and friend was a guy named Tapti Gray, aka Apache.

These two teamed up in 1990 and attempted to burglarize a warehouse that stored explosives. Neither of them would talk to the police, so officials could only speculate at the time what the two wanted to do with the stuff. With this information, I contacted the Los Angeles PD; and although everyone who worked on the case is long retired, I tracked down one of the investigating detectives. He told me that both Payne and Gray are tough customers. He tried every trick in the book during interrogation to get the two to crack or turn against each other, and got nowhere.

Now, here's the interesting part. He told me that while Payne and Gray were doing time in Folsom Prison, they always hung out with a guy named Peter Graves. Who is Peter Graves, you ask?" Not waiting for an answer, she went on. "Peter Graves was long suspected as being part of the Burrowing Bandits, who in 1989 tunneled under a bank's vault in Los Angeles and stole over $172,000."

"Hey, I remember that case," said Tim. "But I thought it was still unsolved."

"It still is unsolved. Graves never admitted to being part of the bank job. He was doing time for possession of stolen property and arson not related to the tunneling. However, rumors on the street suggested that he was the mastermind behind the bank heist; but, now that he's dead, we'll probably never know." With that, Darcy stopped to see if anyone had questions.

"Darcy, did you get any more information about the actual bank job?" Jeannie asked.

Looking at her notes, Darcy replied with the following: "The group was later labeled by the media as the Burrowing Gang, consisting of an unknown number of suspects. The L.A.P.D. estimates that it took a group of people at least several months to tunnel in from a sewage tunnel under the First Interstate Bank of Los Angeles vault. Best guess is that there were at least two suspects. Using drills, picks and shovels, they tunneled until they got within 5 inches below the vault. The vault was time-locked and couldn't be accessed quickly by bank employees without drilling into the vault themselves. The bank manager and assistant manager were actually in the building on days that the under-vault drilling was taking place, but they had no reason to suspect anything.

Our Los Angeles office took over the investigation and immediately felt that despite being expert tunnel diggers, the thieves were obviously naïve to bank robbing since they didn't bring along proper tools to rip open the safe deposit boxes.

The robbery had seemingly been planned to correspond with the Memorial Day weekend when the bank would be closed, giving the suspects an extra day to go after the boxes. But again, they didn't bring the right tools. The evidence left behind suggested that the 100-pound drill they used had unexpected issues: the diamond studded drill bit continually slipped and wouldn't tear through the vault's 18-inch-thick concrete floor. It looked like the robbers had to spend an extra week chipping away at the vault floor with concrete saws and hand drills in order to finally break through.

The police measured parts of the tunnel and found areas to be no larger than three by three-feet, with rounded corners to avoid a collapse. The chamber they created directly beneath the vault was four feet wide and five and a half feet tall. The investigators followed the tunnels and found another chamber twelve foot high. That chamber had been used to tap into the bank's power supply so the thieves could use power tools to dig. Marks on the walls showed that lanterns had been placed every twenty feet or so. All told, the tunnel was about one hundred feet long. The investigators estimated that the robbers had to make roughly 1,500 trips with wheelbarrows full of dirt to get rid of about 3,000 cubic feet of earth." With this,

Darcy closed her file and looked at everyone in the room. No one spoke for several seconds.

Finally, Jeanne summarized what they had just heard: "OK, now we know that the drawing our informant saw was showing a sewer system leading to an area near the bank. Thanks to Darcy's research, we know one of the suspects and a possible accomplice. We know the *how*. They plan to tunnel under a bank and enter the vault from underneath. The *why* is good old greed. The *when* will be Christmas Day. Payne definitely has the experience of going underground, and if we assume that Apache is in on it as well, they have the advantage of more experience. Now we just have to figure out how far along are they."

CHAPTER NINE

It was almost 10 p.m., the day before Christmas Eve when the men began walking to the exit of the sewer system. "So far, so good," said Apache to Two-step. "This time tomorrow night, plus or minus, we should be inside the vault drilling away."

"Yeah!" Two-step replied, "And with some luck, PG&E will cut power throughout the city as they install new transformers--causing even more problems for the cops. Hey, look guys, make sure you have an alarm clock or something to keep track of the time in case you lose power at home. I want everyone ready for me to pick up by 8:30 p.m. tomorrow--a little earlier than I told you before. Got it?" he asked.

Receiving an affirmative from Apache, Jimmy and Blackbeard, Side-step told them that once the job was complete, they would go to his residence, divvy up the currency and conduct a more detailed survey of the loot, then contact the fence so that they could get their money as soon as possible. His main concern was Jimmy, the meth-head. Apache and Blackbeard would stash most of their earnings away and initially spend it sporadically so as to not draw attention to themselves. But Jimmy would snort and shoot it away as fast as he could, even though he said he would not. He had killed several VCs in the tunnels of Cu Chi, but killing Jimmy would be his first since then. Yet, it was something he was contemplating for himself, Apache and Blackbeard.

The group each grabbed a broom and began brushing the dirt and debris away from the tunnel entrance in case someone saw footprints and decided to investigate. Satisfied that their presence had been erased from the ground, they decided to grab something to eat at Denny's.

Once inside, the group found a booth away from the main door and waited for the waitress. After placing their orders, Two-step asked Apache what he was going to do with his earnings from the bank job. His main purpose for asking the question was not to hear Apache's response, but to study Jimmy and read his body language. Apache said he was going to invest again in mutual funds like he did after the last job. He named some of the funds and their yearly returns.

"Smart man," said Two-step when Apache finished. Looking at Blackbeard, he said, "And you?"

Blackbeard joked about buying things in his eBay and Amazon carts, but then got serious. "No, I'm going to put some of it in the market, some in gold, and the rest in several money market accounts--all in under $10,000 increments."

"Why don't you just put all of it in one bank?" asked Jimmy.

"IRS!" Blackbeard said. "Those assholes have the banks notify them when anyone puts in $10,000 at one time--even drug dealers know that. Shit Jimmy, you put all the money you get tomorrow night in a bank or credit union and all the fucking bells and whistles go off with the IRS who will come-a-knockin' asking you where you got the money. Those fuckers are worse than the cops. Not only will they put you in prison, they'll sue you for back interest."

Two-step could see that the warning Blackbeard gave Jimmy went in one ear and out the other. He decided not to ask Jimmy what he was going to do with his share. He had to take Jimmy out. The question was when and where. He knew that Apache would understand why Jimmy had to be killed. In fact, if Two-step asked him, he would do it in a heartbeat. He wasn't sure about Blackbeard. Working in the coal mines creates a bond much like he had with fellow tunnel rats like Apache. But once it was done, what could Blackbeard do about it--especially after Two-step and Apache explained the necessity. It had to be done as soon as the bank job was over, and before Jimmy got any of the spoils.

The foursome split up after leaving Denny's, with Apache and Two-step walking back to their vehicles.

Blackbeard and Jimmy said goodnight and drove off together. “We have to take care of Jimmy you know,” said Apache.

“I know.” said Two-step. “Right after we leave the bank.”

Jimmy walked to his parked black Indian FTR motorcycle and started it.

He thought of the various ways he could kill Two-step after the bank job while putting on his helmet. Not for the money, just for revenge. He still had not figured out why Lorraine, the girl of his dreams, visited the Federal building.

CHAPTER TEN

VATICAN CITY

The pope received word from the office of papal travel that his trip to San Francisco was scheduled to begin on the morning of March 8th, culminating with his presentation to the faithful at the Holy Virgin Cathedral where its golden onion domes rose above the pastel houses of San Francisco's Richmond neighborhood. In the cathedral, the largest Russian Orthodox cathedral outside Russia, he would speak of the need for the two religions to come together as one, something that has not been considered since the Great Schism in 1054. This would take place at 1:00 p.m. on Sunday, March 10th.

At 83 years old, the pope has said many times that he does not particularly enjoy traveling, but he is a committed globe-trotter at an age when previous popes ease-up and tend to stay inside the Vatican walls. Trips have been a testament to his physical endurance; but they also show the pope's sense of urgency--nearly seven years into his papacy--at a time when his voice has seemed to lose ground to more nationalist sentiments around the world.

His trips no longer commanded the global attention they did in earlier years. Instead, they have been quieter affairs by papal standards--often voyages to small countries on the Catholic periphery where he has highlighted issues at the center of his papacy: the acceptance of migrants, environmental protection, and outreach to the Muslim world. All of these issues collided with the beliefs of the current United States president.

The pope of course, has problems in his own backyard. The Vatican is still consumed by the sexual abuse crisis and is dealing with financial scandals, along with a long-standing effort to revamp its bureaucracy. But the pope from the beginning of his papacy made it clear that he wanted to push power within the church away from the Holy See--taking the faith to what he has sometimes described as the "peripheries." It is in some of those peripheries, too, where Catholicism is growing more quickly, and his travels show how the church's center of gravity is shifting away from its historic European base.

Of course, he would not be flying alone. His entourage and security detail, not to mention the large press group that would accompany him, would affect how easy (or difficult) it will be for him to get around.

Code named “Shepherd One” by papal staff in reference to Air Force One, the pope does not have his own plane; the Vatican arranges for him to fly on an Alitalia charter. Actually, the code name for the flight by Alitalia Airlines is AZ 4000, and in Italy, it is simply the "papal flight," or *volo papale.* The flight would take him to Detroit where he would later transfer to a United Airlines jet.

Alitalia's papal flights used to be accompanied with greater pomp and circumstance. Those accompanying the pope would receive wine, perfume, chocolates and more; however, now the flights approximate that of any other charter. Payment for the pope's charter flight is subsidized by the press corps who join him on his flights to cover his activities, and who sit in coach. Getting in-air access to the pope and his entourage is why paying business seat prices for uncomfortable coach seats is worth it to press members.

In years past, the Pope-mobile evolved continuously, with car models progressing from Range Rovers, to Mercedes-Benz, to Fiats. The cars have become decidedly less luxurious (Mercedes-Benz was a previous favorite) since the new pope was selected.

For this trip to the U.S., the pope knew he would be transported in a modified Jeep Wrangler according to the Vatican. The top of the jeep would have a protective cover, but the sides would be open. He eschewing a protective glass-encased ride because he did not want to be shut off from the people. Of course, his penchant for close proximity to his flock created headaches for his security detail; but, for the most part he got what he wanted.

He also learned that the president of the United States would be in San Francisco on that date, but he made no attempt to schedule a meeting with him since, with the exception of respect for the offices they held, their pollical ideology were diametrical opposed. Espousing the merits of socialism was something that many Catholic faithful did not share with the pontiff, but they continued to attend church services in spite of their differences. Not so with the president of the United States. Advocating open borders and condemning the detention of illegal aliens, there was an almost immediate confrontation between the two as their war of words was broadcast by the media. He recalled questioning whether the president was a Christian and received a response which labeled him a disgraceful religious leader for questioning a person's faith. "No." he thought. "There will be no meeting with the president on this trip."

CHAPTER ELEVEN

"Good morning, Mr. President," said Tom Peterson.

"Good morning Tom. Hell of a game last night. The Forty-niners were kicking the Seahawks butts until the damn injury bug took out several of their key players. Before that happened, it looked like it was going to be a rout. I think those two teams will square-off in the NFC Championship game. Mark my word."

"Yes, and I think that once the Niners get those key players back and face Seattle in their home stadium, things' will end up a lot differently. What were the odds that they'd lose their starting tackle, wide receiver, center, and running back before the end of the first-quarter?" said Tom.

"I think you're right. This looks like the year the five-time Super Bowl champions could return to the 'big show,' as they say. So, what's on the agenda today?" the president asked.

"Well sir, first the good news. The polls, even from the fake news agencies, have you up by 13-points over any of your Democratic challengers. The conservative agencies give you a 16-point lead. I really think that the rallies you've been holding in those purple states are putting fear into the liberals when they see the huge number of people attending firsthand. My advice, even though I'm not your political advisor, is to continue these events as we get closer and closer to November. Most Independent voters have swung your way, being upset over the radical left that seems to have taken over the Democratic Party."

"Actually Tom, I had this same discussion with both Laurie and Jason and that's the plan. To tell you the truth, that's one part of the job that I actually love to do--to feel the energy created by those supporters in these arena-filled events. Well hell Tom, it's not a secret, I feed off of them. But I don't want to be like the Niners last night and go into the election thinking I have it in the bag, only to have something come out at the last minutes to shoot me down, so to speak Those assholes have been coming after me even before the day of my election. What else do I have today?" he asked while helping himself to a second cup of coffee.

"Laurie and Jason have given me the dates for your future rallies. One is slated in Arizona, another in Nevada, and the last is in San Francisco," Tom said. "They'll be setting up more as we watch the polls, and we'll target those states that might be up for grabs."

"San Francisco. That ought to be fun for my Secret Service team. I wish voters who for some reason are still undecided could think back and remember how gorgeous San Francisco was before the damn liberal democrats came in there and started instituting their left-wing ideology. Hell, I attended a Super Bowl hosted by Stanford University in 1985, I think. Not sure of the date, but it was between the Niners and the Miami Dolphins. Joe Montana versus Dan Marino. My dad took me as a chance for us to bond and also to get out of the damn cold in New York. He decided we should stay in San Francisco, so we went out there a few days before the game. We went to Pier 39 and had clam chowder and sourdough French bread, then took the boat out to tour Alcatraz Island. Hell, we got to experience what solitary confinement was like after a park ranger put us in a cell." The president paused while looking out of the oval office window.

"He got a cab--no Uber in those days--and had the driver drive down Lombard Street. We visited China Town, the Wax Museum, Knob Hill and the Presidio. The next day he took me to Golden Gate Park, the Planetarium, and the Hall of Science. Everything was so clean compared to the grime and crap on the streets of downtown New York City.

I went out there three years ago and was shocked. The downtown area is filled with homeless people, drug addicts, aggressive panhandlers. People would pull down their pants right in front of you and urinate and defecate on the street. Do you know that the city actually pays people who make almost $100,000 a year to go around and pick up human waste, and then wash-down the sidewalks?" The president did not wait for an answer and continued. "A lot of the San Francisco police officers I talked to off the record said they were trying to get on with some other departments since their administration and district attorney have handcuffed them from doing their duties. To top it off, it was one of the first sanctuary cities I think; but San Francisco is not the only place the damn democrats have screwed up. Look at Los Angeles, Baltimore, and New York. Hell." He stopped and sipped some more coffee.

"Shit, San Francisco. That damn state hasn't voted republican since what, Arnold Schwarzenegger got elected governor? But I guess Laurie and Jason have a reason, so I'll go. What date will I be there?" the president asked.

"March 10, sir," Tom replied.

"Well, at least it is not March 15th," the president replied.

"Why is that sir?" asked Tom.

"That would make my visit to San Francisco on the Ides of March and that didn't go over well for Julius Caesar," the president remarked.

The three jihadists checked into a Motel 6 in Burlingame, California. The two-star motel was an upgrade from their normal living conditions in Libya. Each got his own room to avoid suspicion. After getting settled in, Khalid and Saif went to Abu's room where they examined a motel provided telephone book. Although the book was dated, they quickly found listings for two scuba diving shops in the vicinity. Saif and Abu would visit the shops separately to purchase the required equipment for their assigned task. Khalid would go to a boat rental office in San Francisco, and the three would meet later that evening at a local mosque where they would receive any late information from the al Qaeda leader.

The second jihadist team consisted of three Saudi's, two males and one female. They arrived at the San Francisco International Airport from British Airways flight number 5951 operated by Aer Lingus. All three were in their 20's and dressed like wealthy Middle Eastern college students and blended in with the other passengers. The female, 5'2" Alilta Shammas, wore her long black hair cascading down her back and held hands with her pretend 5'10" boyfriend, Mustafa Haddad, who had a two-day's growth of facial hair. Her blue pullover sweatshirt and loose-fitting black pants could not hide the striking body she attempted to conceal. The third member, Anwar Nafti, was the tallest of the three, standing at nearly six-foot and carrying more weight around his middle than Mustafa. Sporting a soccer team baseball hat and carrying a blue Nike backpack, he ignored eye contact with the other two as they walked through the airport towards the taxi-waiting area. They were in no way ready for the cold and foggy conditions that awaited them upon exiting the airport. The three stopped outside before hailing a cab, opened their carryon luggage, and grabbed light-weight jackets--there being no need for a heavy jacket in Saudi Arabia.

Climbing into a taxi they told the driver to take them to the Marina Inn, a two-star motel near Pier 39. They were unaware who had made the reservations for them, but when they checked-in they found that Alilta and Mustafa would be sharing a room, while Anwar had a single. After Haddad visited the mosque in the morning, they would get-together to receive further instructions.

"As-Salaam-Alaikum," said the male greeter at the entrance door to the large four-story mosque.

"And to you my brother," Mustafa Haddad replied.

"Please, follow me," the greeter said as he began to climb the stairs located to the left of the front entrance. Haddad followed. After climbing three stories, the greeter knocked on a closed door.

"Unkhul," (enter) came a male voice from behind the closed door.

Haddad entered and saw the Iman sitting on the floor outside a larger room used for communal prayer on Fridays known as jāmi‘. The Iman rose and extended his hand to Haddad for a brief handshake. "Come my brother. Let us go to a better place and talk," he said. Haddad followed him up to the fourth floor and into a small room. During the climb to the fourth floor, Haddad saw that the city mosque layout was similar to other mosques he had visited. He saw an ornamental niche called a mihrab set into the wall that indicated the direction of Mecca (qiblah), an ablution facility and a minaret from which calls to prayer were issued. The pulpit (minbar), from which the Friday sermon (khutba) was delivered, was a lot larger than what he had seen in Saudi Arabia.

The man motioned to a cloth-covered chair, directing Haddad to make himself comfortable. "My brother, Allah has given you and your team, Alilta and Mustafa, the great honor of conquering mortality. You and Mustafa will receive seventy-two virgin maidens in paradise as a reward for your sacrifice to Allah, and Alilta will once again, meet with her husband killed by the Americans last year. Everything in paradise awaits you all."

"Allah 'Akbar," Haddad said.

The Iman stood from his chair and walked to a desk located near the far wall. He took out a manila folder and handed it to Haddad. "This is your mission. As you see, the leader of the false church in Rome will be in San Francisco on March 10th attending a meeting with other false religion dignitaries--here in this church," pointing to the Russian Orthodox building. The Iman told Haddad it would be impossible to gain entrance into the main cathedral, but if he and his team could blend into the overflow crowd, the result would be almost as deadly. You three must scout out the area and find the most effective locations for your task. I will leave that up to the three of you."

There was a knock on the door and the male greeter entered carrying three large backpacks. Haddad knew what was inside each bag and therefore did not examine the contents.

"My brother, Allah is waiting for your actions. Make sure it is completed on March 10. Should you hear of other strikes taking place before yours, do not concern yourself. Fulfill the mission God has given the three of you. You will soon be in paradise."

CHAPTER TWELVE

Jeannie briefed the SAC on the information she and her team had received about an apparent plan to tunnel under a bank and commit burglary.

"How are you going to find the exact bank?" SAC Mark Lomax asked. Lomax had been recently appointed to his position after Jeannie turned it down and requested to be the Assistant SAC instead. Lomax knew he was second choice and admired Jeannie's honesty and integrity for admitting that she wanted to learn the "ropes" before becoming a SAC, especially in the politically charged liberal city of San Francisco. The two worked well together, although their investigative styles were radically different.

After graduating from the University of Southern California with a Master's degree in statistics, Lomax joined the Los Angeles Police Department. He rose through the ranks of the LAPD where he served for 15-years before joining the FBI. He started in the patrol division, spent three years in undercover narcotics, and finally made detective. Because of his analytical mind and decision matrices, he was promoted to the robbery-homicide division where he received high marks from his superiors.

Lomax loved to collect data--the more the merrier—and was known as a "grinder." Before taking the San Francisco SAC job, he was known in the LAPD for having a desk covered with spreadsheets, files, graphs and charts. Always neatly dressed and opting for the business casual look, he allowed the agents under his command to dress more contemporary. He married his high school sweetheart and together they had four children. As an owner of a non-descript brown Honda Civic, he could not understand how Jeannie could justify paying over $70,000 for a car made out of fiberglass. He did not drink or smoke--just the opposite of Jeannie's former life.

Jeannie, on the other hand, was a "connect-the-dots and react" investigator. Whereas Lomax was content thinking inside the box, Jeannie was more comfortable thinking outside the box, and occasionally destroying it. She worked her way through the education system by first attending Chabot Junior College in Hayward, California, then transferring to San Jose State University where she majored in Criminal Justice. She completed her BA degree at the University of San Francisco. During two marriages and working at various Lucky food stores, she managed to not only earn two master's degrees in psychology, but also a doctorate. Very few co-workers knew she had a Ph.D., although they should have come to that conclusion if they knew she had been trained at the Quantico behavioral science unit.

Unlike Lomax, she did not marry her high school sweetheart. In fact, she was so busy playing girls' softball and wrestling that she did not have time for any real relationships in school. She did not attend either her junior prom or senior ball. She had a few male friends that took care of her needs, but nothing that developed into anything of a serious nature. Her parents emphasized the importance of college and that there would be plenty of time for relationships once she landed a job in her field. Attending a career day event at USF, she attended a presentation by a female FBI agent. That was all it took. The presentation convinced her that she was born to be an FBI agent and serve her country. She graduated first in her class at the FBI training academy in Quantico, Virginia and was on her way.

After being shot in the Roseville field office, Jeannie told herself that the incident was a wake-up call to clean-up her lifestyle. No more drinking until passing out and no more one-night stands, awakening next to an unknown individual in the dark. The new Jeannie rarely if ever drank, and if she did, she had one and was done. She started attending the gym regularly and rewarded herself with a brand-spanking new red 2020 Corvette. The crowded freeways in the bay area made it impractical to have a car that could go from 0--60 mph in 2.8 seconds, but she found it nice to know that she could. On trips to her cabin in Coeur d'Alene, Idaho, she had plenty of opportunity to let her rip.

In her home workroom she covered the walls with notes, crime scene photos, possible suspects, etc., and then strung lines of string from old-fashion thumbtacks to knit people and events together. She also loved to pit one suspect against another and watch how things shook out. Her preference was to solve a case and then let people like Darcy prepare professional looking matrices for court. Sometimes she called her work "style-organized chaos."

Lomax, as well as Jeannie, were part of the house-cleaning going on in the FBI, removing remnants of the Obama administration appointees after allegations of FISA abuse and spying on the president-elect. Both Lomax and Jeannie knew it would take some time for the overhaul to be complete, but for the first time in a long while they and other "working" agents felt that the president and the attorney general were covering agent's backs.

"I have Darcy working with the city engineers in locating possible tunnels that could give the suspects close access to banks downtown, focusing on our informant's bank first," Jeannie said, and continuing, "The big problem is that the sewer system in this city is about as up-to-date as the Alcatraz Prison underground. The sewer plans go back to before the 1906 earthquake. They've been modified so many times that the engineers are hoping the informant's bank is the intended target; those plans are the most accurate. If that's the best bet, then as soon as possible I'll have a few team members dressed as sewer department personnel conduct a few "normal" inspections in the early morning hours, checking for signs of traffic. If we luck out, we'll start round-the-clock surveillance and catch them in the act. It's supposed to go down between Christmas Eve and Christmas Day."

"Hell-of-a-way for you to spend Christmas Jeannie. Sounds like you covered all the bases. Good luck and keep me posted," Lomax said while reaching to answer his phone.

Jeannie returned to her team's meeting room and noticed that someone had brought in a few pizzas and sodas. "Boy, that smells good. Thanks to whomever brought lunch." Looking around the room she noticed that everyone was there except Darcy. Before she had rime to ask where she was, Darcy walked in with a stack of papers. Placing them on a large 3' by 12' table, she unfolded a large map showing the sewer systems of greater San Francisco. "Looks like you've been busy, Darc," Jeannie said, as most of her team busily grabbed paper plates, napkins, and pizza slices.

Smiling, Darcy said she had learned more about the city's sewer system than she wanted to know.

"San Francisco's unique in California as the only city served predominantly by a combined sewer system. San Francisco collects both sewage and storm water in the same pipe network, then treats and discharges the combined flows into San Francisco Bay or the Pacific Ocean."

"Yuk!" an unknown male team member yelled out while everyone else except Jeannie and Darcy ate pizza.

"On a typical dry-weather day, the system collects and treats more than 80 million gallons of wastewater, primarily municipal sewage. That's enough water to fill 120 Olympic-size swimming pools. By contrast, during rainy weather the system can collect and treat more than 500 million gallons of sewage plus storm water per day. The city owns and operates, get this, about 1,900 miles of sewer mains and laterals right under the streets. End-to-end, it would stretch from here to Colorado and back. Over 300 miles of it are more than 100 years old." Darcey stopped and looked at Jeannie.

"Well, that seems to really narrow it down, doesn't it?" Ismail said to everyone's laughter.

Looking at Jeannie, Darcy broke into a big smile and said that, in fact, she was able to narrow their search down considerably. "OK, Darcy. Grab some pizza before everyone else eats it and tell us the good news," Jeannie said, grabbing a slice for herself and some soda.

Darcy finished her pizza and took her map to the white-board in the center of the room. Using scotch tape, she secured the large colored map of an area circling a downtown building. Seeing that everyone was watching her, she asked Jeannie if she should report. "We're all yours, young lady," Jeannie responded, causing Darcy to blush since she was the youngest female in the room.

"First, the engineers and I found all the bank locations in the city, including South San Francisco. There are two banks, here and here (pointing to the map) that fit the anticipated crime so to speak, but this one (circling a bank) is the most likely one since it's the bank Berkman works at. It's located near one of those 100-year plus sewer systems which the engineers say are rarely inspected because they're a lot smaller in circumference than the new tunnels--some only measuring 36 inches. They only venture down there if there's a backup during the rainy season.

"Sound like the size of most Vietnam tunnels. That has to be the place," Ismail said.

"Just to make sure, we need to check the other less likely banks also, and cover all bases," Jeannie replied. "I've arranged to have several sewer-inspector uniforms delivered here. Tim and Nina, you two check out the sewer systems for the other bank. Carry a few rakes and bags to make it look like you're doing routine maintenance. When you get to the tunnel entrance, don't go in, just in case you're being watched. Look for footprints, dirt debris; you know, signs that someone has been there recently. According to the engineer who dropped off the coveralls, the tunnels leading to either bank haven't been inspected in years.

Flores, you and I will take Berkman's bank and check the sewer system there."

CHAPTER THIRTEEN

Tim and Nina arrived outside the old sewer system near the second bank that had been identified by Darcy and the city engineers as a possible target. Dressed in their city inspector clothes, they nonchalantly looked at the ground, attempting to show little interest in what they were doing--just two bored underpaid civil servants passing time on public tax dollars. The entrance to the sewer was about 10' in circumference, and upon entering they saw abandoned grocery carts and wet clothes that had obviously been there for a long time, and heard the scurrying of what they believed were rats retreating deeper into the cavern. The tunnel tapered into smaller and smaller dimensions until one would have had to get down on their knees to proceed farther. Seeing no signs of disturbance to the walls nor any debris, they wrote it off as not being the target and returned to the entrance.

Nina called Jeannie and reported their findings. Jeannie told them to go home and take a shower if they'd like, and to call it an early day since both of them would be working Christmas Eve through Christmas Day.

Jeannie and Ismail Flores drove to the 100-plus year-old sewer tunnel in Flore's bureau car. A light rain was starting to fall, and the wind was picking-up. "I wonder if we're going to have a PG&E outage today?" Jeannie asked.

"You know, I'm thinking about having one of those Generac generators installed in our house. They've had great reviews and it would hook-up to our natural gas line. A friend of mine had one installed, and he had no problem when the power went out last time. Plus, I'll bet it helps when I try to sell our house someday since these power outages seem like the new normal," Ismail said. "What do you think?" he asked.

"Yeah, my neighbors also had one installed a few weeks ago, and they love it. That long five-day plus span of no power caused them to lose over $800 of frozen food in their garage freezer. They both go up to Alaska each year to fish for salmon, and they had their freezer filled to the brim when it happened. God, they were pissed. Around this time of year when family and friends come to visit for the holidays, they would smoke up a whole bunch of salmon that everyone raved about," Jeannie said. "For me, I'm not sure the investment is worth it since I'm rarely home, and when the damn power goes out, I'm content with candles and a flashlight. Probably be different if I had a large brood like you do."

"Hey, here we are," Ismail said as they reached a larger drainage ditch. They parked their bureau car several blocks away from the drainage ditch so it would not be noticed; they did not want to go through the hassle of getting vans from the sewer department. Like the other team of agents, they walked casually towards the sewer as if taking their time at the expense of taxpayers' dollars. Upon entering the long concrete drainage ditch and looking carefully, nothing seemed to be amiss. But, when they made their way to the end of the larger ditch where it met the smaller ancient system, they saw many signs of recent activity: tire tracks, upturned mud, and disposed cigarettes on the ground. Someone had tried to sweep the area, but there were still signs of recent activity. Knowing from the sewer system engineers that no recent work had been done in this tunnel, both Jeannie and Ismail knew they had the right one. They retraced their tracks back to the car, removed their coveralls, and returned to the bureau. Now they knew the *where* and the *when*, but not the precise *time,* nor how many bad guys would be involved.

"Good morning. What are you looking for?" asked the dive shop clerk.

"Hello, I need everything for a dive soon. I need a complete wet suit with hood, buoyancy compensator, regulator, mask, and a tank; oh, and underwatering lighting," Saif said.

"We can do that," the clerk said while mentally calculating the amount of profit he would make from his first customer of the day.

Saif was on the alert for signs that the clerk might be suspicious.

While the sale was progressing at the San Francisco Marina, Abu and Khalid checked on the availability of a week-long boat rental for March 15th. Meanwhile, Alilita, Mustafa and Anwar traveled to 2600 Geneva Ave, Daly City, to take pictures of the Cow Palace, the site of the presidential rally scheduled for March 10th.

CHAPTER FOURTEEN

After the canal visit, Jeannie ordered 24-hour surveillance of both the tunnel and Two-step's apartment. She decided to also check out Two-step's apartment again by herself before taking the Dumbarton bridge home. She thought she should get there before her surveillance team showed up; she would not approach the apartment until the team arrived for back-up. Parking her Vette across from the apartment, Jeannie watched for several minutes. There were no lights on, no cars; no activity whatsoever. Approximately 30-minutues later she noticed a bureau undercover van taking a position down the street from her location. She called dispatch to let that team know she was going to take a walk towards the suspect's apartment. They recognizing her red Vette and knew she was there. Not many agents could afford such an awesome vehicle.

Wearing her navy pee-coat, Jeannie walked across the street. The rain was coming down hard now, and her watch cap was soaked before she reached the walkway to the front of the apartment. Still no noise or activity. As she neared the apartment, she felt in the pit of her stomach that something was not right: just a feeling--nothing concrete. She knocked on Two-steps' door, having a cover story in case he answered. There was no indication of movement from the inside, so she knocked again harder. Still no response. Were the surveillance team not there, she would have cracked the lock and entered the apartment; but that was now out of the question. She decided to try the manager.

"Hi. I was looking for the guy who lives in apartment 29. That prick owes me some money, but he's not answering," Jeannie said to the male answering the door labeled "Manager."

"What guy? Why the hell are you disturbing me?" he asked--obviously pissed off.

"Look, I'm sorry I woke you or whatever, but I have two kids at home that are hungry and the guy who lives in number 29 owes me almost $100. Can you let me in to see if I can find some money--I'll give you some of it?" she asked in the best hooker voice she had.

"Get the fuck out of here, bitch. That guy left a few days ago," he gruffly said, slamming the door in her face.

She started back towards her car and did some mental math. "Let's say he left three days ago; that would be December 20. That means he's either living with someone from his crew or has a different place to hang out before the bank heist. They're getting ready to hit the bank on Christmas Eve--Christmas Day! It's about to go down," she thought. Once back inside her car, Jeannie called and cancelled the surveillance team's charge. They hit the high and low beams of their van while executing a U-turn, and left the area. The following night she and her team had to be ready and in place.

Heading towards the Dumbarton bridge, she called Ismail and told him that Two-step had checked out of the apartment. She asked him to contact the rest of the tunneling investigative team and make sure they would be at the bureau tomorrow night by 7:00 p.m. for briefing and deployment. Ismail told her that Darcy still has no lead as to where Apache might be living.

Arriving at her residence, Jeannie began reminiscing about her mom and dad, and how coming home to their house during this time of the season was always so special. Her Mom had the inside of their home filled with the scents of Christmas: fresh baked cookies, her dad's favorite fruitcake, candy, and a carton of eggnog in the refrigerator. Their Christmas tree was always lit from morning until bedtime; and her dad, coming home from his second job, always paused for a few minutes to check on his illuminated outdoor decoration of Santa and his reindeer made of plywood cutouts. He would make sure that when her mom entered the front room, he was standing strategically under the mistletoe to get a warm kiss.

She entered her home, finding nothing resembling her parent's house when she was younger: no Christmas tree, no candy, and God forbid any fruitcake. She wondered how anyone could eat that stuff. Instead, her home was inviting, but lacked anything that would indicate Christmas was near. "Maybe next year," she thought.

Jeannie called dispatch and asked if the two surveillance teams were in place near the sewer drainage ditch. She was told that they were, but no one had not seen any activity. For some reason she automatically said, "Merry Christmas" to the person on the other end of the line and hug up. She assumed her remark must have come from all the reminiscing. Popping a Stouffer's turkey tetrazzini dinner into the microwave, she set the timer and walked to the master bedroom--removing articles of clothing as she went. She removed her bra and put on a San Francisco 49ers jersey displaying the number 16, the number of the Hall of Fame quarterback Joe Montana. A pair of black sweatpants and thick socks provided warmth and comfort.

The microwave timer buzzed and Jeannie went back to the kitchen. She placed the hot dinner on a second plate, grabbed a fork and a can of diet Canada Dry ginger ale and headed to her second bedroom where one wall was papered with information, pictures, and mug shots of Two-step and the Apache. String ran from several pictures to other posted items, creating a spider web design on the wall. "Soon, I'll have you bastards!" she said out loud. She was jostled out of her thoughts when the cellphone rang. She saw it was Ismail. "Hey, what's up?" she said while answering.

"Hey boss, I just wanted to let you know that surveillance just saw Two-step get out of an old van and walk down to the drainage ditch."

"Oh shit! Don't tell me it's going down now," Jeannie said.

"Don't get your panties in a bunch; he was alone. He was down there for maybe 15 minutes and then returned to his van and left," Ismail said.

"Damn, if I would have thought about it, I should have had a trailing car nearby and we could have followed him to his new place," she responded.

"Hey, why waste money and manpower. We don't have anything yet. We'll catch them in the act tomorrow and have plenty of time to determine where they all live. Besides, it's too cold and rainy outside for this Portegee," he said while laughing.

"Yeah, I guess you're right. At least it's confirmed we have the right tunnel. OK, thanks for calling. What are you and the family doing now?" she asked.

"The kids are bouncing off the walls; you know, Santa coming, and all. For me, I'm eating some warmed leftover malasadas with the wife and washing it all down with eggnog. I put a little extra something in my wife's so I might get lucky later," he added.

"No, he didn't Jeannie," yelled Ismail's wife in the background.

"You're terrible!" Jeannie said, directing it to Ismail.

"We'll see you on Christmas Day, right? We'll have a large turkey, a honey-baked ham and all the trimmings. We'll hold off opening presents until you get here and have dinner later in the evening, if that is OK with you," said Ismail's wife.

"I wouldn't miss it for the world," Jeannie replied. "An as for you Ismail, I'll see you tomorrow night. Get a good night's sleep." With that she hung up, not waiting for a response.

CHAPTER FIFTEEN

Christmas Eve meant nothing to Marek, Khalil, or Basem. It was just another day in which infidels around the world celebrated the birth of a false prophet. Soon, they would learn that the one true God is Allah. Marek and Basem took another cab ride to the Cow Palace, leaving Khalil at the motel. Both participated in small talk with their Pakistani driver. Most of the conversation was about soccer and the upcoming World Games. They exited the cab and gave the correct fare plus a tip to the cabbie, and began walking towards Daly City's large indoor arena situated on the city's northern border with neighboring San Francisco.

They knew the president would be staying at the Ritz-Carlton, a five-star hotel that is an integral component of the city and a reflection of it. The symbiotic relationship played out in alluring ways: from luxury suites that command city views, to Bay Area wines showcased at the Parallel 37 restaurant, to the cable-car stop located outside the hotel's front door. A filthy display of western wealth, they thought. Additional amenities included a chic Club Lounge and 24,000 square-feet of stylish event space, but this was too small for the popular president to hold his gathering in hopes of raising more campaign funds. Security would be extremely tight.

With March 10th approaching fast, the two felt the need to spend several additional hours checking out the grounds surrounding the large complex, and where they could kill the most people from outside rather than trying to breach security and enter the Ritz-Carlton. They knew the American president would not be injured in their martyrdom; but by taking as many supporters as possible, Allah would be pleased.

There were several routes to the Cow Palace they could take, depending on their original location. From Highway 280 North from San Jose, or from San Francisco they could take either Highway 101 North, Highway 101 South, and finally, Highway 1 South. None of this mattered to Hakin or Basem. They did not care how the infidels arrived. They just wanted to know where they would be standing when each of them set off their bomb.

Those arriving by car had to exit Geneva Boulevard and slowly maneuver onto Cow Palace Drive which ran into a large parking lot. An Internet search resulted in the following information: "The main building consists of 48,000 square feet separated into bays by pillars 40 feet apart East/West and 20 feet apart North/South. The halls are approximately 345 feet in length by 140 feet wide. The ceiling height is 14 feet with vaulted ceilings." The most important factor was that due to the age of the building, very few entrances and exit sites were available. This meant that the crowd not able to gain entrance would be cramped together outside, watching large television sets broadcasting the events going on inside. In other words, there was nowhere for them to escape.

After taking a few more pictures of the surrounding area of the building, both seemed satisfied as to where each would position themselves on the evening of March 10th.

For the umpteenth time, Jeannie looked at all the photos in her second bedroom. She and her team knew the identity of only two of the players: Two-step and Apache. They knew nothing about the others. She felt the job was too big for just the two of them; but how many additional suspects were there? To offset this unknown factor, Jeannie had two tactical teams on notice who would be in position once the burglary went down. What was she forgetting? Something was bothering her, but she could not put her finger on it. She knew the date, the where, including the location of the tunnel, but not the time. What was she not figuring into the equation? "Enough," she thought as she walked back into her family room where Albert Fenny, dressed as Santa Claus, was singing *Father Christmas* as he pranced down a 19th century street on Christmas Eve. She curled herself under her 49ers blanket and watched the movie to its conclusion, eating a few Christmas cookies she picked up at Safeway. Next to come on the television was Chevy Chase's *Christmas Vacation,* and this brought back more thoughts of her dad. What would tomorrow evening hold, she thought, as she began watching the Griswold's going out into the wild to select the best Christmas tree ever.

CHAPTER SIXTEEN

"Good afternoon Mr. President," said Laurie and Jason, the president's re-election strategy team. "Have you seen the recent poll number, sir?" asked Laurie.

Before the president could answer, Jason chimed it, "You're up 18 points, sir."

The president looked at both of them as they took seats across from his desk. "Yes, I saw them, but I must tell you that all the polls had my former opponent leading in nearly every state almost four years ago. I certainly hope our surveys are a hell-of-a-lot more accurate, that's all."

"Yes, sir. I believe that our numbers are extremely accurate and the turnouts you're getting at your rallies are driving the fake news agencies batty, which is why we wanted to see you," she replied glancing at Jason, indicating he should jump in.

"Mr. President, we have some more details about your planned rally in San Francisco. It will be held at a place called The Cow Palace located in Daly City down the road from the city. The arena seats 11,089 for ice hockey and 12,953 for basketball. But, with our configuration, we should be able to get in just over 15,000 supporters. You're scheduled to be on stage at 6:30 p.m." Talking so quickly and glancing at his notes, Jason did not see that the president wanted to say something.

"Yes, I'm well aware of The Cow Palace, Jason. Do you two know that the Cow Palace hosted the Republican National Convention twice, and that the Republicans gathered at the Cow Palace for the 1956 Republican National Convention to re-nominate Dwight D. Eisenhower for president and Richard Nixon for vice president? The ticket won in a landslide. And, in 1969 my dad took me there to see the Beatles second U.S. tour." The president said, and then turned and looked out the window, obviously remembering something from his youth. Laurie and Jason just looked at each other, saying nothing. "OK. Well, thank you for the update. At least that should be an easy place for the secret service to cover," he said while turning away from the window.

"Yes sir. The secret service was relieved when we notified them of our location of choice. The SFPD will take primary responsibility for the security of individuals outside. Given the capacity of the arena, many will not be able to get in; but we have numerous big screens outside for them to view. Sir, will the first lady be attending this rally?" Laurie asked.

"No, she'll stay here, and when I return, we'll fly to our home to spend the holidays," was his reply. "Too bad. San Francisco was such a beautiful place when I was young," he said as he turned his back on them and returned to looking out the window. Jason and Laurie took that as a dismissal and quietly left the oval office.

Holding hands as directed by the al-Qaida leader, Shammas and Alilta walked in front of the Holy Virgin Cathedral located at 6210 Geary Boulevard. Hoping their behavior had not drawn attention to him, Anwar took pictures with his Nikon 3500 camera from across the street, focusing on the various streets that led to the cathedral. After studying the topography, he felt that most attendees not able to get inside the church would be located on Fulton Street, between Fillmore and Webster streets. Since the cathedral would not handle a fraction of the expected "faithful," the spillover crowds would be standing outside. He smiled as he envisioned the infidels standing with candles while the leaders of the two false churches met. "Allah is great," he said quietly to himself and motioned to the other two that he had what they needed.

Khalid, and Abu met with Saif in his room after they returned from the San Francisco Marina. When they entered, they saw all the scuba diving equipment purchased that day displayed on a bed and two scuba tanks on the floor near the door. "The owner of the store gave me a discount on the second tank, so you (pointing to Khaid) will only need to buy a wetsuit, regulator and these things."

"All went well?" asked Khalid.

"Yes, the shopkeeper was more interested in the fact that I was paying with money," he replied. "I also went to a computer café and printed out material about our target." He spread the numerous papers on the second bed. "Here is where we must attach our explosives."

"Why there? Why not in the middle?" asked Abu.

"The depth is 45 meters there--too deep, my brother, for you and me. This spot is only 13 to14 meters, and the damage will be equal in that location. I do not anticipate problems, but should we have any, we can stay down longer than at 45 meters."

CHAPTER SEVENTEEN

Jeannie awakened at 7:35 a.m. to the sounds of a garbage truck lifting up cans and emptying them in their truck as it worked its way down her street. "Shit!" she thought, "I should have remembered to put it out last night." She quickly jumped out of bed, grabbed a light overcoat and ran to the side yard to get her garage and set it curbside.

"Hi Jeannie," said Delores, the neighborhood gossip and Jeannie's next-door neighbor who was standing in her oversized bathrobe, fluffy slippers and hair in curlers. "Sometimes those guys come very early, and other times not until late in the afternoon. What are you going to do?"

"Hi Delores, how are you?" asked Jeannie, who really didn't care what kind of answer she got back, while steering her garbage can to the curb.

"Oh my God, I've been so busy, you know with Judy and her Girl Scouts activities this time of the year, and of course, she's in ballet. Have you heard the latest from our homeowner's association?"

"No, I too have been really busy at work. What are they up to now?" Jeannie asked.

Jeannie wasn't a big fan of homeowner's associations. She understood some of the rationale behind having a homeowner's association—to make sure homeowners took pride in their yard and house maintenance; but some can be overbearing, creating more and more restrictions and acting like "big brother."

"Well," Delores said. "Several of us received letters stating that we were in violation of some type of rule that prevents us from hanging up Christmas lights outside our homes. Can you believe that?" she asked. "How could anyone be offended by Christmas lights and decorations?" she asked, as she looked at Jeannie's house and noted the lack of any sign suggesting that the Christmas season was upon us.

"Sadly, that's the type of world we seem to be living in," Jeannie said. "What are you and the others going to do about it?" she asked.

"Since it's so close to Christmas, we can't file a grievance since the board doesn't meet until next year--you know, January. So, what we decided to do to 'voice' our dissatisfaction was move all of our outdoor lights and decorations inside. Huh! No one's going to tell me I can't celebrate Christmas in my own home."

"I agree with you. Even in the bureau we seem to be walking on egg shells when our staff decides to decorate the offices for Christmas. Everyone's afraid of offending someone. Did you ever see the movie *Last Ounce of Courage*?" Jeannie asked.

"I don't think so. Is it any good?" Delores responded.

"I really liked it, but you know how conservative I am. It's a story about a veteran Vietnam war hero who loses his only son in Afghanistan. His daughter-in-law was pregnant at the time, and after giving birth she moves away with the grandson for 12 years. When they return to spend Thanksgiving and Christmas, the grandson questions why no one celebrates Christmas like they used too? He'd seen home movies of his father growing up decorating their house, having a Nativity scene--you know, decorations everywhere. Well, the grandson's questions fires-up his grandfather who's also the part-time mayor of the fictional town."

"God, I think I like where this movie's going," said Delores.

"Anyway, the mayor decides to decorate the town for Christmas the way it used to be done, including a large Christmas tree in front of city hall. But, just like our homeowner's association, some bureaucrat from Washington D.C. sees a television spot showing the mayor decorating the town for Christmas, and creates a confrontation that involves the separation of church and state. The bottom line of the film is that Americans have stood by for too long and let many of our freedoms erode away simply because of a vocal minority who say they're offended. You should check it out. I think you'd like it," Jeannie said as she tried to retreat back to her cozy abode.

"What did you say the film was called? Maybe I can pick it up at Red Box," said Delores.

"I don't think you'll find it there; it came out in 2016 or 2017. The film's called *Last Ounce of Courage.* You might have to buy it on Amazon or eBay," said Jeannie as she reached her front door, hoping to escape Delores's grasp.

"OK, great! Thank you. By the way, don't forget to let us know when you'll be heading up for Idaho so we can take care of your garbage can and watch-out for your house," she said as she walked down the driveway.

"Thanks, and I will as soon and things slow down at work. It won't be until February or so, but I'll definitely let you know. Have a Merry Christmas if I don't see you before the big day," Jeannie said as she entered the sanctum of her house, away from her pesky neighbor who means well, but sometimes drove her out of her mind.

Jeannie glanced at her watch; she had spent over thirty-minutes talking to Delores. She needed to get dressed and hit the stores so she could buy Christmas gifts for Ismail's kids and a house gift for him and his wife to take when she joined them for Christmas dinner. "Nothing like waiting until the last minute," she thought. "Oh well, it should be fun, but hectic."

Phoning dispatch to see if surveillance had anything to report, she was told that the suspects show up each night at the same time, 11:30 p.m., stay for approximately five hours, and then leave. It appeared to be their SOP (standard operation procedure). She planned on attending St. Edward's Children's mass at 4:00 p.m. It was called the Children's mass since some of the Catholic school kids perform a rendition of the Nativity, and are then invited to sit near the altar while Father Lynch asks them questions about why we celebrate Christmas. Their answers can be hilarious, and that afternoon's mass would probably not be an exception. Jeannie got there in time, and during the celebration she tried with all her might to get her mind off of what she anticipated later that evening, but to no avail. "Do I have all bases covered?" she repeatedly asked herself.

Before receiving communion, the priest invited the congregation to ask for special intentions in silence--which Jeannie did, praying to God that none of her team would get hurt during the evening, and that the unborn child she lost in the shootout was in God's hands. She decided to leave mass early so she would have enough time to grab something to eat, buy goodies for her team members during the briefing, and get home to dress for the stakeout. She smiled while thinking of the special intentions asked by the congregation that evening, and how hers was totally different.

CHAPTER EIGHTEEN

Jeannie backed the Corvette out of the garage, and using the garage-door opener waited for the door to close. There was a light mist and everything smelled especially fresh, prompting her to a recall all the Christmas Eves she had enjoyed during her life that smelled the same way. She called Ismail and told him she was on her way to the bureau, and asked if there was any new information that had come in about the suspects. Receiving no additional intel, she hung up and prepared to hit the Fast Lane as she approaching the Dumbarton Bridge. Her grandfather on her dad's side of the family had helped build the bridge back in 1927. He would probably roll over in his grave if he learned that people were still paying to use the bridge in the 21st century.

The Dumbarton Bridge is not much of a bridge when compared to the other bridges in the area. After numerous updates, the current bridge included a two-way bicycle lane and a separate pedestrian path on the south-facing side. A 340-foot center span provided 85-feet of vertical clearance space for shipping. The center spans were twin steel trapezoidal girders which also supported a lightweight concrete deck. The bridge is the southernmost highway-bridge across San Francisco Bay, carrying over 70,000 vehicles and about 118 pedestrian and bicycle crossings daily, and is the shortest bridge across the bay at 1.63 miles. Its eastern end is in Fremont, near Jeannie's home in Newark in the San Francisco Bay National Wildlife area, and its western end is in Menlo Park. Of course, it does not visually compare with the grandeur of the Golden Gate bridge or the Bay Bridge.

Once off the bridge, Jeannie headed north on U.S. Highway 101 and arrived at the bureau office at 2030 hours, approximately 90 minutes before everyone else assigned to the investigation were to arrive. She bought a decorated Christmas cake, Christmas cookies, sodas, Christmas cups and dishes, and a box of mixed See's candy to place on the large conference table for all to enjoy when they arrived. "God," she thought, "I remember buying a whole one-pound box of See's candy for ten dollars. This three-pound box was over a hundred. Hope everyone enjoys them." The thought brought a smile to her face, thinking that her mom and dad would have thought she was crazy to pay so much for candy.

More and more agents began arriving in addition to her team, all helping themselves to the refreshments.

Most were wearing blue windbreakers with FBI stenciled in yellow on the back, but Tactical team members were dressed in black battle-dress uniforms with bloused combat boots. She invited Darcy to attend, not only to help her feel like a team member, but because her research got them to this point in the investigation.

"First, I want to thank everyone for being here on Christmas Eve. Sorry, the bad guys don't seem to be traditionalist and celebrate the holidays like we do." Everyone laughed, with a few hoisting their soda cans as a toast.

Jeannie removed the dark plastic cover that Darcy had placed over the large smart-board. There were pictures of Two-step and Apache at the center of the board. To the right was a picture of the Bank of America building as well as several aerial pictures that showed street locations, sidewalks, and adjacent buildings. "This is where the action's going to be," Jeannie stated as she pointed to a concrete canal leading into darkness.

Jeannie, Ismail and Darcy talked everyone through all the developed intel. Jeannie added, "The only problem Ladies and Gentlemen, is that we don't know how many bad guys we'll be dealing with tonight. These two (pointing to Two-step and Apache) are hardcore; they've served many years in prison. Whether they'll go down peacefully remains to be seen. We've got to assume they're all armed and have explosives.

We'll take up positions at 2130 hours. They've been showing up at 2300 hours each night. We have no intel to know if they're aware we're on to them or not; but, let's assume that when they arrive, they'll check the area out before going into the canal. It should go without saying--please be careful! I want everyone to go home safe and sound Christmas morning so you can see what Santa brought you--except Flores, he's been a bad boy," Jeannie said.

"Hey, wait a minute," Ismail responded, while everyone laughed and grabbed more finger-food.

CHAPTER NINETEEN

Two-step drove while Apache sat in the backseat of the van. Blackbeard was waiting near the side of a 7-11 store while smoking a cigarette, and after spotting the van he threw the remnants of his smoke on the ground and walked towards the van. He climbed into the front seat saying, "What's up?" to no one in general. No one responded as Two-step exited the store's parking lot and headed to the agreed upon location to meet up with Jimmy. In the back of his mind he was still deciding when and where to take Jimmy out. He thought it was probably best to wait until the bank job was complete.

The van displaying the city of San Francisco Sewer Department insignias on its sides was parked near the closest corner to the drainage canal. Each of the four crew members had mining caps with LED lights on their heads as they left the van, and each carried backpacks containing the tools and explosives needed for the job. Two-step and Apache, ever so vigilant about the presence of cops, gave a quick cursory look of the entire area before entering the cement canal that led to their man-made tunnel, followed by Blackbeard and Jimmy.

Jeannie had just finished her briefing and final orders, and was filling a paper plate with salsa, guacamole and chips when she heard Ismail yell, "Shit!" while slamming the phone down on the desk. "Oh shit! The suspects just drove up. It's going down now," he said.

Jeannie looked at her watch; it read 2150 hours. "Why did they change their schedule?" she thought. "Shit is right! she said. "Everyone grab your gear. Here we go--and remember to be safe."

Jeannie and Ismail parked their vehicle in their assigned location. "Unit one, they've been in the canal for over 30 minutes. They've parked their van just west of their location. We snuck-up on the van and it's empty," reported the surveillance team who had the best view of the canal.

"Roger that, unit one," said Jeannie.

"Tac-1 and Tac-2, are you in position?" Jeannie asked.

"Tac-1, roger," came the response.

"Tac-2, in position," was the second response received by Jeannie.

"Now we wait," she said to Ismail.

"The most boring part," he responded.

Jeannie looked at her watch; it was now 2330 hours--just before midnight. "By the way, they've kept to their modus operandi by setting off the alarm numerous times throughout the day. Surveillance said the bank manager is so pissed that when he responds he quickly drives around the bank, calls security on his cell, and then can't wait to get out of the area," Jeannie said.

"Huh." Ismail uttered, and then said, "How much time do you want to give them in the tunnel before we approach?"

"If we go in too soon, we'll only get them for attempted burglary and maybe conspiracy, and in this damn state they would only get a slap on their wrists and community service. Tell you what, what if you and I stroll down by the canal and see what we can observe from that location? We'd be closer than the two surveillance teams. What do you think?" she asked Ismail.

"Anything is better than sitting here on our asses," came his response.

"All units, this is team leader. Agent Flores and I will be taking a walk near the entrance to the canal. Maintain your positions until advised." They got out of the bureau car and began walking towards the cement canal. The wind began to pick up, which did little to help with the fog blowing in from the ocean. Jeannie placed her arm into Ismail's left arm and they began walking slowly towards the location, acting as if they were more interested in each other than what was going on just below them.

"Don't get too excited. You know I'm a married man," Ismail said.

"Oh, don't flatter yourself," came the response from Jeannie.

Just then a huge gust of dusty wind blew out of the canal, bringing visions of the dust clouds that blanketed New York City streets when the towers came down on 9-11. "Get down," Ismail said as he quickly grabbed Jeannie's arm and they hit the ground. There was no sound of an explosion, but something had to have caused the dust cloud. They looked at each other while still on the ground, using the street lights behind them for illumination. Both were covered in ash, dust, and whatever. Ismail asked Jeannie if she was alright. She tried to shake off as much dust as possible and said, "Yes."

"All units, they've apparently set off an explosive device. Tac-1 and Tac-2, begin your advance. Your teams will take over from here to the conclusion. Be advised that Agent Flores and I will be retreating from the concrete canal when you make your entrance. Please acknowledge."

"Tac-1 roger."

"Tac-2 roger."

As Jeannie and Flores began to exit the canal, the two Tactical teams heading towards the earthen tunnel entrance passed them. Jeannie and Flores had not completely come out of the canal when shots rang out, lasting two to three minutes. Neither Jeannie nor Ismail could determine the number of shots due to the echo created by the concrete drainage system. Not wanting to tie up the Tactical teams' communications system, Jeannie waited for an announcement. Finally Tac-1 came on the air.

"Team leader, this is Tac-1. We have two suspects down--dead. A third appears to be a causality of the explosion and a fourth is in custody. It is safe for you to advance. Copy?"

"Copy Tac-1. Confirm none of our personnel are injured."

"That is correct Team Leader. Everyone is OK." He continued, "Dispatch, notify the coroner.

Ismail and Jeannie began their approach to the cement canal end, aware of not contaminating any of the evidence that would be collected later. The Tac-1 leader walked up to them and provided a synopsis of what went down.

"As we left the canal, we could hear voices coming from that tunnel," pointing to it with his flashlight. "Pretty good engineering feat for a bunch of thugs," he said. "They had a unit pumping in oxygen, lights on the walls, and re-enforced material to hold up the ceiling. It was really sophisticated. When we moved deeper into the tunnel, we found it partially blocked by a mangled body. It appears to be a male that was dragged out to where we found him. We continued and found body parts all over the walls and floor near the vault floor. The explosion must have taken him out; but after removing him, the remaining assholes continued as if nothing had happened. When we got closer, we heard drilling and small talk, and as we approached the bottom of the vault we could see the hole made by the explosive. It sounded like there were three in the vault." He stopped and took a took a sip of water from a bottle he had in his tactical bag.

"Coming out," said one of two Tactical team members escorting a handcuffed male. He did not establish eye contact with Jeannie, Flores, or the Tac team leader who was escorting two agents to the crime's epicenter.

"Follow me. This is the best way to get to the scene without disturbing the area and creating problems for the crime scene techs. Watch the walls. Somebody decked the halls but not with boughs of holly." "Yuck!" said Jeannie as she and Ismail followed the Tac team leader farther into the tunnel.

About 10 feet from the blasted hole in the ceiling of the tunnel leading into the vault floor, they both saw two bodies. Near each body was a semiauto handgun. One had its slide back, indicating that the gun had emptied its clip. Jeannie immediately identified the two as Two-step and Apache. There were numerous entrance wounds to the upper bodies of both.

One of the tactical team members said, "When we got about here, we called out to the voices inside, announcing our presence. After a hush, the guy you just saw walk out in cuffs, yelled that he was coming out and was unarmed. We took him into custody and two of our team started to walk him out. They didn't get very far because those two (pointing to the dead bodies) quickly jumped down from the hole in the vault floor, firing rapidly during their decent. We opened up and it was over."

"Guess they didn't not want to go back to prison, huh?" asked Ismail not expecting an answer from either of the other two.

They both climbed up the small ladder that was laying inside the open floor to the vault. Jeannie entered first. "Gee, looks like they were well into their attack on the safe deposit boxes," Jeannie said as they looked at a drop-cloth near the hole in the floor filled with jewelry, cash, gold coins and other valuables. Almost one-fourth of the boxes had been drilled opened and their contents emptied onto the drop cloth. They had about a third left to drill when they were interrupted by the Tactical teams.

Ismail looked at Jeannie and asked, "What do you think happened during their final minutes here?"

Jeannie paused, turned and looked at the vault, and then back at Ismail. I think there was an accidental detonation, after which they decided nothing could be done with the victim so they carried on. Well into the crime they were confronted by us, and the third suspect--whoever he is--decided to give up. Two-step and Apache had already done hard-time and probably told each other that going out in glory was better than a return to the cellblock. How's that sound to you?'

"God, you should start writing crime novels. You'd be good at it."

"Oh, shut up! Let's get out of here so the coroner and the crime scene unit can do their jobs."

Jeannie called dispatch on her personal cellphone, requesting that the SAC be briefed so he would not be blind-sided before Jeannie could go over the events in detail. She wanted an FBI spokesperson sent to the scene immediately to handle the press who had thus far not arrived. Finally, she requested that the SFPD send a few officers to help with crowd control once the public heard about the shootout through the media.

Both Jeannie and Ismail waited until the spokesperson arrived. Her name was Sandy and she was really good about saying something that meant nothing. Jeannie told her to keep most of the detailed information close to the vest. She should say that two individuals had been shot and died at the scene, and that they were part of a group of four suspects attempting to break into the bank vault after tunneling under it. One suspect was apparently killed during the explosion and a fourth suspect had surrendered to the FBI and was in custody. That was enough for now, Jeannie told her.

"Got it," said Sandy who, wearing her blue blazer with the yellow letters FBI on the back, wondered off to a site she wanted to use during her media interviews. Right on cue, several vans arrived and cranked up their satellite dishes from the roofs, while reporters made sure their makeup was just right before going on the air.

Jeannie and Ismail began walking back to their bureau car when Jeannie heard someone calling her name. She turned and saw Julia, a Fox News reporter and someone Jeannie not only liked but trusted, wave to her and motion whether she could approach the two of them. Jeannie and Ismail had little respect for those in the news media, referring to them as "fake news vultures." Jeannie waved her over.

"Hi Julia. What brought you out here on Christmas Day?" Jeannie asked as both she and Ismail shook her hand. "As if we don't know!"

"Believe me, I was in bed with my boyfriend and started cursing when the network called. What can you share that those assholes over there aren't going to get from Sandy?

Ismail looked at Jeannie and said, "Go Boss. You're better at this than I am."

Jeannie told Julia that there were four burglary suspects involved in the attempted heist of the Bank of America. "They'd been digging a tunnel from the main concrete canal for months, finally reaching a site directly under the vault. Using a yet to be determined explosive, they blew a hole in the floor of the vault, but in the process, one of the four was killed. Once they entered the vault, they began drilling the safe deposit boxes for their contents. When confronted by our Tactical teams, one of the suspects immediately surrendered, but the two remaining decided to shoot it out, dying in the process. Those two had served hard-time in prison. To our knowledge, none of the property stolen by the suspects left the vault, and it will be the bank's task to determine the rightful owners. That should do it for you Julia."

"Thanks Agent Loomis, as always, if you need anything at all, don't hesitate to call." With that, Julia walked to the area where her colleagues were being briefed by Sandy so her camera crew could take pictures of the scene.

"I think we're done here ace," said Ismail, and the two headed to their vehicle.

CHAPTER TWENTY

By the time everyone returned to the briefing room, with the exception of the agents involved in the shoot-out, it was 0130 Christmas morning. Jeannie thanked everyone for a job well done and asked them to make sure their reports were promptly submitted when they returned from the Christmas holiday. She knew her team already had enough prima facia evidence in their submitted reports to legally hold the in-custody male over the holiday break, but she and Ismail would interrogate him before calling it a night anyway.

His name was Matt Castro. He waived his Miranda Rights and was in a frantic talkative mood; it would be reasonable to say that he just wanted to get things over with. He was from West Virginia and had been a coal miner with Jimmy Wyatt, the name of the guy blown up in the vault explosion. He said that the four of them, under the leadership of Two-step, had pulled off a similar job in West Virginia. It was a small bank and they really didn't get much for their efforts. Using the same method as this job, Two-step would find a weak-link in the bank from either a female teller or a bank employee/manager who had a weakness for drink. He would milk them for all the information he could, and them drop them cold.

He discussed how Two-step got the information from Lorraine, although he did not know her name. They had hoped to get at least a million dollars out of this job. Jimmy, he said, had a meth habit and all three of them were becoming concerned about Jimmy running his mouth.

Castro continued, "Tonight, everything was going like clockwork, except we didn't know you guys were on to us. Two-step set the fuse for the explosive and told us to leave the area. Then, for some reason, he told Jimmy to go back in, and you know, give everything one last look. Shit, Jimmy was kind of out of it on meth and just did it. Then, wham, the damn explosion occurred. Jimmy, or parts of him, were everywhere. I don't know what happened. There must have been something wrong with the fuse. Man, I was so confused; I didn't know what to do, but Two-step and Apache remained calm and dragged Jimmy down the tunnel, away from the vault. They returned and Two-step looked at me and said that Jimmy would have wanted us to complete the job, so we did." With that, Castro stopped speaking and looked at his cuffed hands. "You know, Jimmy was a good guy, but he got that poison in him and it eventually took him over."

"How long have you guys been working on the tunnel?" Ismail asked.

"Maybe three months, more or less," was the response.

"Damn, you guys were good moving all that dirt, reinforcing the walls and ceiling, the lights. I have to tell you--we are all impressed. Too bad the four of you couldn't have found a more non-criminal enterprise to use your talents," Ismail added.

"Yeah, well, you know. Things just happened," he responded. He didn't know where Jimmy, Apache or Two-step lived--only their general locations. The location he had for Two-step was a no-go since it was the apartment Jeannie and Ismail visited and found vacant.

He could not provide information about where the explosives came from, nor what they were planning on doing after they completed the job, other than refraining from spending any of the money until Two-step told them it was OK. Figuring they got as much useful information from him as they could, they had him taken away, and they too called it a night. Jeannie made a personal call to the SAC and gave him all the information she had up to that moment. He congratulated her on a job well done and wished her a Merry Christmas.

They took the elevator down to the security garage and Ismail walked Jeannie to her Vette. "We'll see you tomorrow afternoon, yes?"

"Wild horses couldn't keep me away," she said.

"See, if you don't want to be a crime novelist, you could go country. Good night, Boss."

"Good night Flo, and Merry Christmas," Jeannie said as Flores walked to his personal car.

"You too," he said, as he closed his car door.

Chapter Twenty-One

While driving home across the bridge Jeannie thought she should be dead tired, but the adrenalin rush from the evening's event had secured itself in her body. Feeling famished, she was fortunate to find a hamburger drive-thru still open on Christmas morning and ordered the largest burger, fries, and chocolate shake they sold. She would feel guilty when she woke up later in the morning, but it felt good to her going down.

Surfing the television channels, she settled for bouncing back and forth between *Home Alone,* where the bumbling burglars attempted entry into Kevin's booby-trapped house, and

A Christmas Story, just before Ralphie opened his gift containing the Red Ryder BB gun. Somewhere in the process she fell asleep on the couch in the same clothes she wore that evening.

Around 9 a.m. Christmas morning, she awakened to the vibration of her cellphone in her front pants pocket under her. She rolled over, pulled out the phone and saw that it was the bureau.

"Loomis," she said.

"Merry Christmas, Jeannie," said an excited Darcy on the other end of the line.

"Merry Christmas to you, Darcy. You didn't have to call me so early to tell me that," while she looked at her wall clock and noticed that it was then a little after 9:00 a.m.

"Oh no, I'm sorry if I awakened you, but I thought you'd want to know that we've positively identified Jimmy. His name is James Wyatt, age twenty-three, and born in West Virginia. The team you assigned to search his house came up with a treasure trove. This guy was obsessed with Lorraine. He had a whole shrine displayed in his bedroom, including the ceiling. He'd been stalking and taking pictures of her for a long time, including her comings and goings from Two-step's former apartment. They also found an enlarged picture on his kitchen table showing Lorraine leaving our building. It was stamped with the date corresponding to the time she came in and spoke with you. He'd drawn a large red question mark over the whole photo."

"Huh!" Jeannie uttered as she tried to get her head around this new information.

"Also, I talked to one of the bomb squad technicians who told me that it appears someone deliberately shortened the fuse on the bomb, causing it to detonate quicker than anyone expected except for the one who did it. What do you make of that?" she asked.

"Well, I think there's a lot of follow-up work we need to do after Christmas. By the way, why are you still at the office?" Jeannie asked.

Instead of answering the question, Darcy said, "We also got confirmation through prints that Matt Castro is, in fact, Blackbeard. He has no criminal record. The Bureau of Mines back in West Virginia confirmed that both he and Jimmy Wright worked at two coal mines together. I just stopped by the office to pick up a present for a friend that I'd left in my desk last night. I'm going with him to his parent's place for dinner and gift openings."

"Way to do Darcy. Sounds serious."

"No, he's just a friend--at least for now. Who knows? Well, I'll let you go. Merry Christmas, Jeannie."

"Merry Christmas to you, Darcy."

Jeannie rolled over and tried to get back to sleep, but that was not going to happen. "Not too many loose ends to tie up," she thought. She could hear kids on the street in front of her home riding their new bikes and scooters to the encouragement and handclapping of their parents. "Oh well, Scrooge, Merry Christmas. Time to get your cute ass out of bed, Agent Loomis."

Following a tradition she shared with her dad, and as her mom had done for years, she cut up a link of linguica, fried some hash browns and eggs, and toasted two pieces of whole wheat bread. She was on her second cup of coffee before everything was ready to eat. "Merry Christmas, Mom and Dad. Love you," she said to herself.

Jeannie put the dirty frying pan and dish in the sink and opted for one more cup of coffee. She had turned on the Fox News channel while working in the kitchen and had not paid much attention to what the talking heads were saying, until Julia appeared on the screen and pretty much regurgitated everything Jeannie had given her at the scene. She heard something about the pope planning a visit to San Francisco at the same time the president would be there for a fund-raising event. "Boy I bet the SFPD is excited about that!" she thought.

Without much effort, Jeannie found a *Celtic Woman* Christmas album and inserted it in the CD player. She removed the center piece from her dining table, and then retrieved ribbons, bows and Christmas paper from her upstairs closet. She grabbed scissors and tape from a kitchen drawer and began wrapping gifts for her visit to Flores' house to celebrate Christmas with his family. She surprised herself when she unconsciously started singing along with the songs.

After completing the wrapping, she showered, dried her hair and selected a red pants suit to wear for dinner. She gave herself a once-over in the mirror, and satisfied with her looks loaded the presents into her car—which, she realized, was not easy for someone who drives a Corvette: space is limited.

The Flores's residence was a Christmas masterpiece. Even Jeannie's dad would have been impressed with the Christmas lights Ismail had placed on the outside of the house. Flores had so many inflatable decorations that Jeannie had to do a double-take to see them all. There was Frosty the Snowman, Santa, Rudolph, Snoopy on his decorated dog house, and numerous deer with moving heads. A Nativity scene completed the display with a sign that read, "Jesus is the Reason for the Season." The darkening rain clouds and limited daylight helped Jeannie imagine how beautiful the house looked at night.

"If you take a picture it will last longer," said a chuckling Ismail who had opened the front door and was watching Jeannie.

"Flo, your house if breathtaking. My dad would have loved it," she replied instead of returning with a wise-ass comment.

"Yeah. Not bad, huh, for a Portaguee? Get in here and take off your coat."

"Come here and help me with the presents," Jeannie said.

"Yes Boss, I'm coming," said Ismail.

Flore's kids ran to the door and helped Jeannie and their dad put the presents under the tree. Jeannie then turned and walked into the welcoming and loving arms of Ismail's wife. They exchanged cheek kisses and she followed Ismail's wife into the dining room where an assortment of finger-foods were displayed.

"Oh my God, malasadas!" Jeannie said gleefully as she grabbed one and reached for a napkin.

"Ismail, get Jeannie a cup of coffee. Here Jeannie, sit here," his wife said, and she schussed her kids who were off the wall since with Jeannie's arrival, knowing that gift-opening was about to happen. Knowing that, Jeannie quickly ate the donut--although she could have easily eaten another--drank her coffee and walked to the family room where she made a comment about all the presents under the tree.

Ismail's oldest daughter, Loretta, took her job as Santa Claus seriously, trying to make sure everyone got a present, had opened it and had showed it to everyone before she passed out another. Jeannie could see that Ismail was a proud papa.

The kids loved the presents Jeannie had given them. Each came over and gave her a hug while thanking her. Ismail and his wife had sworn to Jeannie that only the children would get gifts; but as usual, the last present under the tree was a gift from their family to Jeannie. Opening it, Jeannie began to cry. Somehow Ismail had secured photos of Jeannie during various stages of her life and photos of her mom and dad, then had them transferred to a digital frame that displayed each picture about every five seconds.

"How did you get these photos?" Jeannie asked, looking at Ismail.

"Hey, I work for the FBI and that's classified," he answered. She gave him a big hug as well as his wife, and then excused herself to touch-up her smeared makeup.

CHAPTER TWENTY-TWO

Dinner was great. Ismail's family had prepared roast turkey, Jeannie's favorite, as well as a honey-glazed ham, mashed potatoes, yams, dressing, peas with little onions, corn, homemade rolls, and the best gravy Jeannie could remember eating. There were so many desserts that Jeannie had a hard time deciding which to choose. As a compromise she took small portions of everything. Stuffed, she realized the next day's gym workout was going to be a bitch.

Jeannie helped clean the table, carrying everyone's plates to the kitchen. She and Ismail's wife loaded the dishwasher while engaging in small talk. Their smallest child fell down and wanted mother's attention, leaving Ismail and Jeannie alone in the dining room to discuss work.

Jeannie started: "I got a phone call early this morning from Darcy. She'd stopped by the office to pick up a friend's present she'd forgotten to take with her last night. They identified Jimmy from his fingerprints on the one full arm they found. He met and worked with Matt Castro in the coal mines of West Virginia. Never married and no kids. Small criminal record, mostly petty stuff. But when they executed the search warrant on his house, they found a shrine dedicated to guess who? Lorraine!"

"What, our Lorraine?" he replied.

"Yup," Jeannie said while nodding her head.

"Nothing incriminating turned up at Apache's residence. Did you know he was highly decorated during the Vietnam War?" Not waiting for an answer, Jeannie went on. "Got an honorable discharge, but when the reccssion hit several years ago, he lost his job, family, and turned to drink. Of course, we know he did time with Two-step, and that's when they came up with the bank-job plan.

At Two-steps house they found more detailed maps and drawings of the plan for the bank heist--but nothing we hadn't already figure out. Sad to see two war heroes go down the wrong path. We'll know more after Christmas regarding bank accounts, phone records, type of explosive used, where it came from……but the thing that's really sticking in my craw is the Jimmy, Two-step, Lorraine triangle."

"Yeah, I was thinking about that myself," Ismail said. "Here's how I see it. Jimmy first saw Lorraine at a KFC, right? Jimmy instantly gets the hots for her, but Two-step must have hurt his ego and made him feel small in front of her. Jimmy gets pissed-off, and while he's thinking of ways to get even, his infatuation with Lorraine grows into a full-blown stalking routine—thus, the shrine in his house. Two-step somehow gets a sense of Jimmy going to strike out at him, and he rigs the explosive to go off early in the tunnel, taking Jimmy out. What do you think?"

"Seems to connect all the dots, but I guess Jimmy and Two-step took their secrets to their graves and we'll never know," Jeannie replied.

Ismail's wife entered the dining room. "Hey, you two, enough business talking. It's Christmas. I have pumpkin pie with Cool Whip, some malasadas, and a berry pie. What do you two want?"

Jeannie had a great time with the Flores's. She really did have a nice Christmas after all. Before leaving she asked Ismail if he would like to swap vehicles in a few weeks--her Corvette for his Ram truck. She wanted to visit her cabin in Idaho, and with snow of the ground a Vette is not the ideal vehicle to drive. "Hell yeah," came the excited response. "Just let me know with enough time that I can arrange to get babysitters for the kids and take a spin down to Monterey with the wife."

Jeannie arrived home with Christmas dinner leftovers that Ismail's wife had packed for her. It always seemed that warmed-up leftover turkey, dressing, mashed potatoes and gravy tasted even better the following day. She wasn't sure why, but after parking the Vette in the garage, she decided to enter her house through the front door. There, at the base of the door was a package that obviously came from See's candy store; it was address to her from Delores and family. "Way to go Delores," she thought as she opened her front door and laid down the box of candy with the other items. "Yes, it was a great Christmas."

CHAPTER TWENTY-THREE

Immediately upon arriving at the bureau, Jeannie checked the SAC's office but found it vacant. In fact, she was so early that very few agents and staff were in the building. She entered her office and found several "While-You-Were-Out" notices which she quickly examined, throwing requests for interviews from news agencies in the waste basket. There was a request from the shooting board to contact them. This was standard procedure since she was the person in charge of the tunnel investigation. She called their number and scheduled an interview after lunch. They asked her if Ismail was also available, and she said that more than likely he would show up with her.

Ismail arrived and checked in. He told her that he and Darcy rode up in the elevator and that she had a lot of new information about the explosive used and where it came from. ATF was offering their services to do all the follow-up regarding this and the firearms used by Two-step and Apache.

"Sounds good to me," Jeannie said. "Give them a call back if you can, and give them everything we have. By the way, we've been requested for an interview by the shooting review board today. We can go together if you're free--say 1300 hours."

"Sounds good. I'll track you down around 1230, OK?" he asked. She gave him the OK sign and went back to looking through the stack of paperwork that had accumulated on her desk regarding issues other than the tunnel case.

By 1000 hours the SAC arrived, walking directly from the elevator to Jeannie's office. Her door was open, but he knocked before entering. "A late Merry Christmas," he said as he put his overcoat and umbrella on one of two chairs across from Jeannie. He then placed a box of See's candies on her desk with a smile.

"You didn't have to do this," Jeannie said as she acted like she could smell the assorted chocolates through the unopened box. "I'll bet they're dark chocolate almond. Right?"

"Gee, you really are a good FBI agent," he responded.

Jeannie opened a bottom drawer of her desk and pulled out an obvious bottle of alcohol. "This is for you--for those days when you feel you're coming down with a cold," she said as she handed it to the SAC.

"Better be Grey Goose," he said.

"Gee, that's why you're the SAC," she responded.

He laughed, stood up and retrieved his coat and umbrella. "Do you have all the loose ends tied-up from the bank job?" he asked.

"Pretty much. The AFT has offered to take over the investigation of the explosive used as well as the handguns. I have several individuals, as well as Darcy, tracking down cellphone usage, bank records--the normal paper trails. I've received several requests from the local media as well as major cable channels for interviews which I'm trying to dodge for now," Jeannie said.

He broke in, "You know my feelings about those assholes--a bunch of bleeding-heart liberals acting as the mouthpiece of the Democratic party. They know nothing about balanced journalism. Tell you what, let me handle the interviews. I like getting into their faces."

"Sounds great to me. Also, I wanted to request a few days off so I can run up to my cabin in Idaho. Of course, that will be after we have the entire tunnel affair wrapped up with legal," she said.

"Shit! You earned it, Jeannie. Take a whole week, and if you feel you need more, give me a call. By the way, the Mrs. said to say Merry Christmas."

"Tell her Merry Christmas from me also," said Jeannie as she left.

Jeannie assembled her team in the briefing room at 1100 hours. This included the two Tactical teams and support staff plus Darcy. "OK, everyone. I want to go over everything we have so far on the bank job and make sure we'll have a complete case for legal by this Friday."

Each individual gave an update on what they were completing, or still needed to follow-up on. By Jeannie's estimation, the case was nearly complete, so she felt that planning her trip to Idaho could start the following Saturday. Ismail showed up at her office as planned, and the two headed upstairs to a smaller conference room where they were individually interviewed by the shooting board. Since neither had any first-hand information about the exchange of gun fire in the tunnel, they both fielded questions about the intel they provided for the Tactical team members. At the conclusion, Jeannie and Ismail hit a local Subway sandwich shop where they compared notes about questions they were asked, agreeing they had come away with the same impression: it was a clean shoot.

"I checked with Lomax this morning and he gave me the OK to take at least a week off so I can head up to Idaho. Are you cool with taking over while I'm gone? I think you heard at the briefing that the tunnel case is nearly wrapped up," Jeannie said.

"Hey, just give me the keys to the Vette and you're out of here," Ismail said, smiling ear to ear.

CHAPTER TWENTY-FOUR

Jeannie walked over to Delores' house and knocked on the door. Delores' son answered, and upon seeing Jeannie screamed to his mom that Jeannie was there.

"Hi Jeannie," said Delores, wearing the same bathrobe she had worn a few days earlier, with her hair still in curlers. "My God! Was that you and your team that was involved in that shootout at the bank?" she asked.

"Yes. Sadly it ended with the taking of two lives, but we think they wanted to end their lives this way instead of going back to prison.

"Well, thank God you didn't get hurt," Delores said.

Jeannie told her she was heading up to Idaho, and asked if she would take care of her garbage can and look out for her house while she was gone, explaining that she wasn't sure how long she would be gone--maybe a week or two. Delores said it would not be a problem and to have a safe trip. She also told Jeannie she had ordered the movie, *Last Ounce of Courage,* from eBay and hoped to get it soon.

Jeannie exchanged keys with an excited Ismail and drove his truck to her house, planning to leave for Coeur d'Alene, Idaho, the following morning early. The main reason she wanted to be away from the area was to avoid all the partying and social gatherings up to, and including, New Year's Eve. She had avoided all alcohol and pretty much cleaned-up her act after being shot.

She was prepared for the nearly 15-hour drive to the lake, deciding to make it a two-day drive instead of driving straight through, with a yet to be determined motel stop on the way. She had recently joined an audiobook club and had several books to listen to during the long drive. She had been listening to a John Sanford's *Prey* novel titled, *Gathering Prey.* Sanford's hero was Lucas Davenport, head of a fictional law enforcement agency called the Bureau of Criminal Apprehension based in Minneapolis. She enjoyed Sanford's style of writing, and the book's narrator had an awesome voice.

When she tired of *Gathering Prey,* she removed the CD and replaced it with a totally different style of writing, *The Covenant of Genesis,* by Andy McDermott. McDermott had made use of his screenwriter-turned-novelist talent while writing it. While listening to his book, Jeannie felt she was in a movie cinema watching an adventure film along the lines of *Tomb Raider*.

"Hey Boss. Where are you?" Ismail asked when Jeannie answered her cell phone.

"Just left Highway Eighty heading east, and now I'm on Highway Ninety-three out of Winnemucca, Nevada," she replied. "I've been driving about six hours now, and I may stop for a late lunch/early dinner before finding a motel. How's everything going?" she asked.

Ismail said, "Great. The shooting board ruled it a clean shoot. He's telling the prosecutor's office everything they want to know. They've offered him a sweet deal for his cooperation, and if he goes for it, he'll get the minimum joint time. AFT found that both guns were stolen from two separate home burglaries, but nothing at the scenes of those two homes incriminated either Two-step or Apache. The explosive was stolen from a mining firm back in West Virginia, so it probably involved Jimmy or Blackbeard , but again, there's no evidence directly pointing to them. The bomb squad said that someone, probably Two-step, did modify the fuse that blew poor Jimmy away. Pretty much everything is done and this is ready to be put to bed."

"How's my car? Jeannie asked.

"Just a few scratches and a minor dent in the rear. Other than that it's fine," he said while trying to suppress a laugh.

"Very funny buddy. Your truck is fine if you wanted to know," she fired back. "By the way, I think I get better gas mileage on my Vette than you get with your Dodge."

Ismail retorted, "Yeah, but think of how much more macho you feel when you climb into that cab."

"Good bye, Flo. I'll call you tomorrow when I reach the cabin." With that, Jeannie signed off.

She found a Carl's Juniors off an exit where she gassed-up. Before she got out of the truck her attention was drawn to a new model black Mercedes Benz. A male and female were putting-on wigs, which is usually not a good sign. She grabbed her purse that contained not only her badge, but also her weapon and waited. The male got out of the Benz first, followed by the female. Jeannie estimated their ages to be mid to late-twenties. The female was wearing a designer pants suit which Jeannie thought might be a Givenchy or Gucci brand that could have carried a $1500 price tag--just for the coat. The male was also a fashion hound. Although not knowing much about current men's fashions, she did recognize that the overcoat he was wearing was a camel hair trench coat, much like the one her first husband purchased from Neiman Marcus for over $2500. A Brioni brand she thought. They pulled out separate duffel bags from the back seat of their vehicle and walked towards the restaurant. Pulling out her cellphone, Jeannie began video-taping their actions surreptitiously. Jeannie waited until they got close to the side entrance door before getting out of the truck and following them.

Instead of approaching the counter to place an order, the two headed to their respective bathrooms. This far north, even in California, one is unlikely to find a "gender neutral" bathroom. "Huh!" Jeannie thought. "Could they be planning to rob the joint?" However, their actions seemed strange for a quick holdup. Instead of placing an order, Jeannie took a booth, placing herself a position to view both the bathrooms and the counter area. Acting as if she were searching for something in her purse, see could see the two came out of the bathrooms, the male first. Their transformations were unbelievable. Wearing dirty jeans and torn shirts, they looked at each other and then left the restaurant carrying duffle bags that undoubtedly contained the clothes they were originally wearing. They seemed to have applied makeup to make their faces appear dirty and distressed.

Jeannie changed positions to a window seat where she could continue to film the two as they opened their vehicle's rear doors and stored their bags. They then began to walk up the exit ramp towards the freeway. Jeannie left Carl's and walked up to the Mercedes and took a picture of the license plate. She looked inside the car but only saw the two duffle bags. "Obviously scammers," she thought. She returned to the restaurant and asked for the manager. A young Latina came from a side office and asked Jeannie what she could do for her. Jeannie told her about the two individuals using the restaurant's parking lot and bathrooms to rip people off for money as they preyed on charitable people. The manager did not seem too concerned about what Jeannie told her, but her eyes opened wide when Jeannie flashed her FBI badge. She told Jeannie she would call the local police.

Jeannie quickly ordered a hamburger, an order of fries, and a small diet Dr. Pepper, and began walking back to her truck. She climbed inside, and from her vantage point she could see the two individuals working two sides of the exit and entrance ramps. "Assholes," Jeannie thought as she got progressively madder seeing charitable people stop and give money to the two. She did not want to waste time watching their activity or waiting to see if a law enforcement officer would eventually arrive, so she did the next best thing. When finished, she climbed back into the cab, started the engine and began driving out of the parking lot while listening to *The Covenant of Genesis.* Before exiting, she took one more look back at the beautiful new Mercedes Benz with four freshly slashed flat tires. "I doubt that the money you assholes scammed today will pay a fraction of what those tires will cost you," she said to herself as she smiled and turned onto the freeway, flipping-out the male panhandler.

The trip to her cabin was exactly what a shrink would have probably recommended after a $150 per hour bullshit session. Coeur d'Alene, a city in northwest

Idaho, is known for water sports on Lake Coeur d'Alene, plus trails in the Canfield Mountain Natural Area and Coeur d'Alene National Forest. The population swells from approximately 50,665 year-round residents to over 100,000 in the summertime. Jeannie thought she might take in the annual Holiday Light Show that would continue until the first of January. In the meantime, with the temperature at 46 degrees, she joyfully took in the city sites as well as buying groceries for her stay. There was no snow expected until the next day, so she did not have to worry about getting someone to install chains on Ismail's truck.

After purchasing groceries and firewood, she headed to the cabin. She was able to purchase the cabin when a local realtor informed her that it was going into foreclosure after its owner, Frank Silva, disappeared. This is the same Frank Silva that she and her team had been investigating in connection with a planned theft of the mythical Ark of the Covenant, supposedly located in a small chapel in Ethiopia. Spending days after the close of escrow searching every nook-and-cranny for hidden evidence or information regarding his possible location, she finally told herself to move on with her life and just enjoy the gorgeous cabin which was slightly over 3,800 square feet. The first thing that caught her eye when she entered the cabin, and before making an offer, was the massive floor leading to a two-story rock fireplace and the exposed log walls and ceiling.

Jeannie, like her parents, loved a roaring crackling fire--even if it were contained in a woodburning stove insert--versus one of those flip-the-switch fake gas-jobs that lacked ambiance. With this thought in mind, she started a fire before getting dinner ready. In the process of making the spaghetti sauce, she called Ismail to let him know she had arrived. The only new information he had to tell her was that Blackbeard would be pleading-out instead of going to trial. Jeannie thought that pretty much concluded the tunneling bank-job case.

In the semi-darkness of Khalid's motel room, he and Abu practiced maneuvering and placing a fake explosive devise around a large plastic garbage can lying on its side. Although the plastic bag was nowhere near the dimensions of their real intended target, they both felt it necessary to practice in the dark to simulate the visibility they would encounter under water. Saif kept track of their progress with a stop-watch, each time getting better at the attempt. March 15th was approaching, and they would be prepared.

CHAPTER TWENTY-FIVE

Reaching her office floor, Jeannie checked-in with her secretary, Tami, who greeted her with her normal big smile and stack of While-You-Were-Out notes. "Welcome back! How was Idaho?" Tami asked.

"Great," Jeannie responded, as she quickly perused them--sorting out the more urgent from the others. She found one that was interesting. It had come from the head of Counter-Intelligence in Quantico and was marked "urgent." Jeannie handing it to Tami, asked her if she knew anything about it. Upon examining it, Tami said it was not in her handwriting, that it was not there when she went home the night before and that she found it on her desk that morning. She had no idea who left it.

Just then, SAC Jim Lomax exited the elevator and saw Jeannie talking to Tami. "Did you get the urgent note from Counter-Intel?" he asked while walking to his office.

"Yes sir. Just found it, and we were wondering where it came from," Jeannie said.

"Sorry if you couldn't read my writing; it came from me. Let's grab a cup," he responded. Jeannie gave the rest of the while-you-were-out notes to Tami, indicating she would pick them up when she finished with the SAC. Lomax and Jeannie walked towards the cafeteria, with the SAC asking Jeannie how her trip to Idaho had gone. Jeannie replied that Idaho was great and thanked him for the time off, and then switched to the subject of the San Francisco Giants' chances in the new year. Sadly, she felt it was time for the Giant's management team to cut some of the loved aging players loose so prospects from their farm team could move it. The SAC seemed to agree, saying it would be sad to say goodbye to a lot of players who helped the Giants win three World Series trophies in five years. He purchased coffee for the two of them and said he needed to discuss the note in the privacy of his office.

"Well, we had a great ride this year with the Forty-niners though," he said as he opened the door to his office. Jeannie found no need to respond.

He allowed Jeannie to enter his office first and closed the door behind him. He walked around his desk while removing his trench coat and hung it on an oak clothes rack.

Taking a sip of coffee and placing the paper cup on his desk, he told Jeannie that before addressing the Counter-Intelligence memo, he wanted to bring her up to speed on the purging that was taking place in the bureau.

"Jeannie, I'm afraid and ashamed to admit that the deep state appears to have infiltrated the bureau up the its highest ranks. That would include the former director whom the president canned. The president is now taking heat from the House of Representatives who earlier despised the former director. Confidentially, there will be more former Obama appointees removed from their current positions. It'll start with the replacement of the Attorney General. My advice to you is to continue flying below the radar until the dust settles. You're a flaming star going to high places in the bureau if you can stay out the shit that's coming down the pike." He paused and took a sip from his cup.

"Thank you for the heads-up," Jeannie said as she reached for her cup of coffee, not really knowing how to respond.

"No, you really have to keep this in the back of your mind while you're working with some of these assholes that haven't been weeded out," he said. "This Counter-Intel memo I left for you is going to put you shoulder-to-shoulder with some deep-state members in the bureau, as well as the National Security Agency and Department of Home Land Security."

"NSA, DHS! Gee, what are they expecting"? Jeannie asked.

"Jeannie, your resume is very impressive. You've kept your nose clean and risen through the ranks the hard way--the way it used to be before politics entered the bureau. The only area where I see that you lacking is in the area of terrorism, both domestic and foreign. Our own division of counter-intelligence used to handle these investigations, but after the screwups on 9-11—well, we now have the NSA and DHS. The NSA is now primarily the analytical arm of the NSA although they won't admit it. They intercept phone calls, Internet usage, and so forth; and if they feel it's warranted, they pass it off to the DHS who actually has agents on the street.

That's why I wanted to brief you before your flight out to Washington, so you have some background information before you arrive. Eighteen years have passed since the terrorist attacks of 9/11, and al Qaeda is worse for the wear. The terrorist organization looks remarkably different today than the group that killed thousands of U.S. citizens on American soil. Intensive counterterrorism pressure in Afghanistan and Pakistan has left behind an aging and increasingly disconnected central leadership. The emergence of the Islamic State as a peer competitor, meanwhile, has left al Qaeda with a brand that, at times, has struggled to compete for global jihadist primacy.

After two turbulent decades following its most spectacular mission, al Qaeda has settled down and is again intensely focused on attacking the West. Following the death of Osama bin Laden and the onset of the so-called Arab Spring uprisings, al Qaeda began to embrace a changed strategy.

Terrorism scholars widely observed that al Qaeda began pursuing more limited strategic goals with a focus on localism and incrementalism. This strategy shift was widely dubbed 'controlled pragmatism' and 'strategic patience.' Al Qaeda seemed to be quietly and patiently rebuilding itself while deliberately letting the Islamic State bear the brunt of the West's counterterrorism campaign. Don't get me wrong. I'm not an expert in this field either, since I left counterintelligence years ago. It's just information I hear from my former colleagues.

As al Qaeda continues to undergo change as a global organization, one of the most pressing questions for policymakers and the bureau, NSA and DHS, is to what extent the group is still focused on attacking the West. Does the absence of a spectacular attack attributed to al Qaeda during this phase represent a lack of capability, or merely a shift in priorities?

My contacts gave me this in 2018," Lomax said as he handed Jeannie a stapled stack of several papers. "It was entitled, '*America is the First Enemy of Muslims.*' We're not sure who authored it, but it incited al Qaeda's followers to start striking the United States again. None of this should be surprising, as al Qaeda's overarching narrative has always been that the West is at war with Islam.

Although the ultimate goal of Al Qaeda is to overthrow the corrupt 'apostate' regimes in the Middle East and replace them with 'true' Islamic governments, Al Qaeda's primary enemy is the United States, which it sees as the root cause of the Middle East's problems. By targeting the United States, Al Qaeda believes it will eventually induce the United States to end support of the Muslim state regimes and withdraw from the region altogether.

Ostensibly in response to intervention by the United States and others in the conflict, Western civilians in the region (including journalists and humanitarian aid workers) have also become targets—though the Islamic State saw them as hostile even before the U.S. intervention. And now that American military advisers are on the ground in Iraq supporting the Iraqi military, the U.S. military has ostensibly become a primary target for the Islamic State, but the lack of troops within range diminishes this danger.

Al Qaeda has long used a mix of strategies to achieve its objectives. To fight the United States, Al Qaeda plots terrorism spectaculars to electrify the Muslim world (and get it to follow Al Qaeda's banner) and to convince the United States to retreat from the Muslim world. The model is based on the U.S. withdrawals from Lebanon after Hizballah bombed the Marine barracks and U.S. embassy there, and the "Blackhawk Down" incident in Somalia. In addition, Al Qaeda supports insurgents in the Islamic world to fight against U.S. backed regimes--and U.S. forces in places like Afghanistan, where it hopes to replicate the Soviet experience. Finally, Al Qaeda issues a swarm of propaganda to convince Muslims that jihad is their obligation, and to convince jihadists to adopt Al Qaeda's goals over their local ones. And that's why you'll be flying to Washington D.C. and attending a major briefing with agents from around the country."

"Why is that? I mean, I understand that we're constantly under threat, and although al Qaeda has, as you said, been quiet for a long time, has something happened recently to move the threat level?" Jeannie asked, already knowing the answer.

"I don't have all the particulars, and that's why you'll be representing the San Francisco bureau and get briefed, but apparently the NSA has picked up a tremendous amount of chatter from the Middle East regarding a resurgence of terrorist attacks here in the U.S. coming from Osama bin Laden," Lomax responded.

"Osama bin Laden? What, has the asshole risen from the bottom of the ocean and re-established himself as Number One?" she asked.

Lomax anticipated her response and said with a smile, "No, I think bin Laden is crabmeat and has been for some time, but apparently something from his past has motivated his followers, and the NSA feels that something big is about to happen."

Jeannie got up to leave when Lomax said, “Oh, there’s something else I need to check with you. I got a phone call from some deputy sheriff in Northern California, at least I think it was in California--doesn’t matter. Anyway, I guess you turned in two fake panhandlers by a Carl’s Hamburger joint.

“Yes, I did. I gave the information to the manager. Did they wrap those assholes up?” Jeannie replied.

“Actually, the deputy called since someone sliced the hell out of tires on the car they were driving. He wanted to know if you saw anything when you were leaving?” Lomax said with a smile on his face.

“Not a thing,” Jeannie said, “But you know what they say about karma!”

Jeannie walked back to her office and called the Counter-Intelligence phone number written on the while-you-were-out memo. The agent who answered had been assigned the task of making sure all representatives from major FBI offices in the nation would be sending a representative. Jeannie acknowledged that she would be in attendance and got pertinent information regarding flight, hotel and transportation logistics so she could give the particulars to the bureau travel department. She would be leaving in two days. “Shit!” she thought. “If there’s one city I hate more than San Francisco, it’s Washington D.C. The president was right when he called it a sewer. If our founding fathers saw how corrupt our government had become, they’d be spinning in their graves.”

CHAPTER TWENTY-SIX

Jeannie called Flores and asked if he was free for lunch, even though it was only 10:00 a.m. They decided on IHOP since Ismail said he would like pancakes. Jeannie opted for a toasted open-faced turkey sandwich, fries, and chocolate shake. She felt guilty, but told herself she would workout harder the following morning with the female drill instructor. She explained to Ismail that she would be leaving for Quantico in two days and that he would take over her position during her absence.

"Lucky you," Ismail said. "Don't comeback all corrupted. Do you want me to take care of your Vette?" he asked with a huge grin on his face.

"No. Thank you. I'll be leaving it here in the garage and have arranged for you to take me to SFO. Unfortunately, I need to be at the airport by 0600 hours, so you'll need to start your day early. Just put in your eight hours and go home early. I'll notify you when I know for sure when I'll be returning.

"So, what do you think? Does al Qaeda still exist, and could they be planning something, or is it just a bunch of bureaucrats trying to justify their jobs?" he asked.

"Shit if I know, Jeannie said and continued: "Lomax still keeps in contact with a lot of the colleagues he worked with while in Counter-Intelligence. I'm telling you--he gave me a quick course in terrorism regarding bin Laden's organization, and I must say I was impressed with his knowledge. He said his friends believe that the chatter the NSA is monitoring gives credence to their concern about a pending attack--so much so, that each large FBI office in the country has been ordered to send a representative. Have you ever heard of something like that happening before?" she asked.

Ismail answered, "I remember there was a lot of scurrying going on after nine-eleven, when people started asking about all the red-flags that were missed. They wanted to know why no one knew in advance about the plane hijackings--and then, the public found out that agencies weren't really 'talking' to each other, even though there was a tremendous amount of chatter about something big about to happen. I mean, all these Middle Eastern males getting on board planes with little to no luggage, and paying in cash. And remember, they had attended flight schools down in…I think it was Florida, and they only wanted to learn how to fly the planes, not take-off or landing maneuvers. A lot of people played Sgt. Schultz, you know, from *Hogan's Heroes:* 'I know nothing, I heard nothing, I saw nothing.'"

"Yeah, that was pretty embarrassing to some; yet as usual, I don't remember hearing about anyone being held accountable for their incompetence," she said.

"Hey, you'll be in the land of incompetence in two days," Ismail replied.

Jeannie once again asked Delores to watch her home during her visit to Washington D.C. Delores could not wait to tell Jeannie that she got *Last Ounce of Courage,* and that she would be requesting that it be required high school viewing at the next school board meeting. "Good luck with that!" Jeannie thought.

Ismail dropped Jeannie off at the SFO departure area in enough time for her to buy a cup of coffee and a Cinnabon. She planned to relax during her flight by listening to an audiobook on her iPhone, having already reviewed all the paperwork Lomax had given her. She felt well prepared for the meeting. If at least one field agent from each of the larger FBI offices had been ordered to attend this briefing, she expected to see over fifty-plus agents. She recalled in her FBI basic training that over 125 FBI, Alcohol Tobacco and Firearms, and U.S. Postal Service agents were involved in the Unabomber--Ted Kaczynski case, but it did not involve ordering agents from all fifty states to attend a special meeting. "This has to be big," she thought as she started her audiobook.

Jeannie waited for her luggage upon arrival at Dulles International Airport. She did not have long to wait, learning a long time ago from her parents that luggage booked late before the plane departs will be the first removed from the plane upon landing. She found an agent who was posing as a chauffeur holding a sign for Ms. Loomis, Mr. Anderson, and Mr. Delgado. When Jeannie approached him, he identified himself as Agent Tom Winters and welcomed Jeannie to D.C. He was in his mid-twenties and was probably low on the totem pole at the bureau, and thus was given the chauffeur assignment. She learned that Agent Anderson and Delgado were also on her flight, and they soon joined Jeannie for the ride to their hotel.

Only brief periods of small-talk took place during the 55–minute drive to the hotel. Nothing was said about the meeting or their expectations. Instead, Jeannie learned that Agent Anderson, a gray-haired man with a trimmed mustache and probably in his forties, was from the Seattle bureau. He mentioned that he had been in the bureau for 15 years. Agent Delgado, sporting male pattern baldness of dark brown hair and wearing glasses, was from Portland. He told Jeannie and Anderson that he had been in the bureau for 8 ½ years, and had recently been transferred to Portland from North Dakota. Both men had flown from their respective states to SFO for the flight to D.C. Jeannie felt that Anderson was a little too liberal for her, but she could not understand why she had that impression. It might have been because Portland has the reputation of becoming another liberal bastion like Berkeley, California. Her dad used to complain that the "left-coast," which included California, Oregon, and Washington, had become so left-leaning that even the liberals who lived there were leaving because the socialistic ideologies practiced by their state legislatures had reduced their states to ones with poverty and homelessness, and with third-world characteristics.

Thank God neither Delgado nor Anderson asked Jeannie to meet later for dinner or drinks; she was tired from the flight and just wanted a hot shower and room service. She turned the iPhone alarm on and connected it to her charger. After watching a little television, she gave in to the tiredness that had overtaken her.

The next morning Jeannie decided to eat breakfast in the hotel restaurant. She knew there would be sweet rolls and other continental breakfast items available in the meeting room before training, but she wanted something more substantial. She saw Delgado's wave to her as an invitation to join him; she said good morning and seated herself at his table opposite him. As the waitress approached their table, Anderson appeared, said good morning to both Jeannie and

Delgado, and took a seat. After the waitress took their orders. Anderson asked if they had information as to why so many agents were meeting at Quantico. After sharing what they had been told, they realized they had received a "canned" synopsis as to why they had been ordered there--it was excessive "chatter" received by the NSA.

Agent Winters arrived on schedule to provide transportation from the hotel to Quantico. It had been many years since Jeannie had attended her basic training there, and she was flooded with memories. Her mom and dad had flown all the way to D.C. to see her graduate top-of-her class. Her dad, a retired police sergeant up to the time of his death, bragged to his former law enforcement buddies that his daughter was an FBI agent.

Winters directed them to the building hosting the meeting and drove off, saying he would return at 3:00 p.m. to take them back to the hotel. Jeannie learned earlier from both Delgado and Anderson that they were told the briefing would end by 3:00 p.m., and that they already had their return flight materials in hand. Jeannie contacted her secretary, Tami, and asked her to inform the travel department that she needed a flight home that evening. The time of the flight did not matter; she just wanted to get home. Tami told her she would text the flight particulars once it was confirmed.

As expected, Jeannie and the other two agents entered the largest auditorium at the FBI training center. Jeannie underestimated the number of agents present; she guessed there were over 100, both males and females. She learned while extending greetings with colleagues that the NSA, DHS, ATF were all in attendance in addition to the FBI. There were others whom she suspected were with the CIA. "Yes, this is big!" she thought.

She took a seat near the front, twelve rows back from the podium and a large overhead screen. About six-minutes later nine individuals, three females and six males dressed in dark suits, walked to the seats behind the podium with the exception of one female who tapped on the microphone to confirm it was live.

"Can you all find a seat please?" she began. "We have a lot of material to cover this morning and hope to get everyone out of here by 3:00 p.m., since I know many of you have flights to catch." She stopped until everyone found a seat and the noise level dropped. Tapping the microphone again to get everyone's attention, she started her presentation.

"Good morning and thank you for setting aside your busy schedule to attend this extremely important and urgent briefing. My name is Adele Stevenson and I'm the associate director of the National Security Agency. Each of the individuals behind me will introduce themselves prior to their presentations so we can save time. Who we are isn't important, but the information we'll share with you is imperative for the safety of our country." Using a wireless presenter she pointed at a Mac Air computer, and a picture of Osama bin Laden appeared on the large screen behind her. She continued, "On May 2, 2011, bin Laden was killed in Pakistan in his compound in Abbottabad (slide advance). (Slide advance) Here are photos taken by Navy SEALs as they secured the large amount of technology taken from the building during the raid.

All total, over 42,000 pieces of technology were removed and taken away with bin Laden's body.

The property was initially taken to NSA headquarters, where for the past eight years most of it has been analyzed for potential intelligence. (Slide advance) Priority was assigned to the devices that had various layers of security--encrypted and so forth—and that pertained to the majority of property seized. However, (slide advance) there were still over 9,000 pieces of technology that were not encrypted and were designated as less important. Recently, on numerous low priority unencrypted devices we found hundreds, if not thousands of possible targets listed by bin Laden--call it his wish list.

In December of last year, we noticed an uptick on chatter originating from Libya, Morocco, North Africa and Saudi Arabia." She turned and walked away from the podium, nodding at one of the two females seated behind her who then took her turn at the podium.

"Good morning. My name is Fahima Saban. I'm the chief analysist at NSA, and as Agent Stevenson just stated, we've noticed a huge amount of new traffic, 'chatter' if you will, primarily emanating from both Pakistan and Libya. All of this chatter contains messages referring to March, two months from now. The trouble is, there's no concrete reference to specific targets."

As if on cue, six males that had been standing to the side of the audience approached a table near the front holding files held together by large colored rubber bands. "Each of you will be receiving a binder containing a list of bin Laden's future targets. As we hand out the binders, take a few minutes to glance at the material and then I will return." With that statement, Fahima Saban walked back to where Agent Stevenson sat and talked quietly with her.

The binder Jeannie received was about a half-inch thick and titled, "Osama bin Laden Forgotten Plans." Quickly thumbing through the binder, Jeannie noticed that each page listed numerous targets: power plants, sewer treatment plants, airports, train stations, cruise ships, sporting arenas, amusement parks, Washington D.C. landmarks, Congress, Pennsylvania Avenue, hospitals, military bases, bridges, dams, tunnels, churches, and on and on. "My God, bin Laden had really done his homework before being killed," Jeannie thought as she closed her binder and waited for Fahima's return to the podium.

"OK, I hope everyone received a binder and had time to review it. I realize there's a lot of information to peruse in such a short time, but let me continue. (Slide advance) As you probably noticed, each state that you agents represent has a number of possible targets in your local. Two months is not much time to make sure these targets are secure. We still have several more devices to analysis, but because of the increase in traffic and the frequent references to March, we wanted to give you the information we've gleaned so far so you can brief the law enforcement agencies in your state who can help investigate these targets.

We at the NSA feel that bin Laden occasionally added to these lists, and that the targets are not in any type of order. We feel he was inspired by what he read on the Internet and devised methods of attacking various sites. (Slide advance) For example: last year's Super Bowl, (slide advance) The World Series, church shootings (slide advance), and private planes that could be used in a similar way to those used on nine-eleven." With that said, she handed the presenter device to a male speaker who followed.

"Hello, I'm Agent Rich Pinheiro and I'm with the Department of Homeland Security." "Hum, this guy is good looking," Jeannie thought. He easily stood six-foot three and had dark brown hair that he wore short and combed back, leaving a little wave that extended over his forehead. Jeannie thought he looked a lot like the San Francisco 49ers quarterback, Jimmy Garoppolo.

Pinheiro continued, "As we worked through those unencrypted devices and started developing these lists, we realized that all of our states have these generic targets, and that it would be physically impossible for federal law enforcement agencies to check out each possible target--and thus, this briefing. While bin Laden was alive, his M.O. was to strike big targets here, and especially abroad: (Slide advance) the 1992 hotel bombing in Yemen, (slide advance) the February 26, 1993 first bombing of the World Trade Center, (slide advance) and the November 13, 1995 car bomb explosion in Riyadh, Saudi Arabia at a facility where the U.S. military was training Saudi National Guardsmen. (Slide advance) In August 1998, Al-Qaeda operatives carried out the bombings of U.S. embassies in Nairobi, Kenya, and Dar es Salaam, Tanzania, killing 224 people and injuring more than 5,000 others, (Slide advance) and in October 2000 with the USS Cole bombing, killing 17 sailors. There are others. (Slide advance) On September 9, 2001 two Tunisian members of al-Qaeda assassinated Ahmed Shah Massoud, the leader of the Northern Alliance, (Slide advance) And, of course, the attacks on September 11, 2001of the Twin Towers, the Pentagon and the flight that fought back until it crashed in a rural Pennsylvania field, (Slide advance) the April 11, 2002 Ghriba synagogue bombing that occurred when a natural gas truck fitted with explosives drove past security barriers at the ancient Ghriba Synagogue on the Tunisian island of Djerba, (Slide advance) the 2002 Limburg bombing on 6 October, 2002, (Slides began advancing quickly) the 2002 Bali bombings, the 2002 Mombasa attacks, the 2003 Riyadh compound bombing, and the Charlie Hebdo shooting in Paris, France on January 7, 2015." He shut off the computer. "The common denominator in all these instances was that they were large-scale attacks intent on killing as many people as possible, and the heck with innocent bystanders. Unfortunately, we (looking back and referring to everyone seated behind him) feel that each of your states could have a target that would fit bin Laden's description of a big event. We have to rely on you and your respective state resources to check out as many of these potential sites as possible between now and March." He glanced at Adele Stevenson and asked her a question that Jeannie could not hear, but it apparently had to do with a lunch break. He told the audience that it would be a good time to break for lunch, and that they would appreciate everyone returning at 12:30 p.m. Lifting up the MAC's lid, a slide showed several states assigned to a particular member of either the NSA or DHS. "When we return, each of these individuals, including me, will be located at the sides of the room. Please, when we come back to session, note whom you will be debriefed by and go to that person's table. We might luck-out and leave early, and avoid traffic. Let's grab lunch." He left the slide on the screen and Jeannie felt her heart leap when she realized that she was in his group after lunch.

The buffet lunch consisted of macaroni or potato salad, French roll with a choice of turkey or roast beef, potato chips, a chocolate chip cookie, and water or soda. Due to the long line of agents, by the time Jeannie got to the buffet table her selection had dwindled to potato salad and roast beef. She grabbed a diet coke and saw that she only had ten-minutes to finish her sandwich and get a seat close to Agent-- "damn, what was his name?" she thought.

Jeannie was the first one seated when Pinheiro approached. He offered his hand and said, "Hi, I'm Richard Pinheiro; but please, call me Rich. You are SAC Loomis, correct?"

Flattered, but caught off guard by him knowing her name and rank, said "Yes, I'm Jeannie Loomis. Have we met?" she asked.

"No, I think I would have remembered you," he said in a flirtatious manner. "I read the case file about the shootout in Roseville. Did they ever catch the suspects that killed your SAC and shot you and the other agent?"

"No. There was no forensics that could help with their identification, and the whole Star Chamber case is cold," Jeannie replied.

"Oh, I would say it's cold," he said with a wink as other agents took their seats.

"I wonder what he meant by that, and was he hitting on me? God, in the old days I could easily tell," Jeannie thought.

"Let's start by each of you identifying yourself and the city/state you represent," Agent Pinheiro requested. Jeannie realized that all the agents in her group represented the west coast and connecting states: San Francisco, California; Portland, Oregon (Anderson's state); Seattle, Washington (Delgado's state); Boise, Idaho; Las Vegas, Nevada; and Tucson, Arizona.

"OK, good. Nice meeting you. You have probably already assessed most of what I'm about to say on your own. For example, in Las Vegas a choice target could be any of the big casinos. Look at the havoc Stephen Paddock caused on October 1, 2017: a lone gunman. How many did he kill, 58?" he asked, looking at the Las Vegas bureau agent.

"Seattle, the Space Needle, Farmers Market, CenturyLink Stadium, to name a few. And, don't you have cruise ships that take passengers up to Alaska?" he asked, getting a nod from the Seattle agent.

"And Jeannie, San Francisco and the surrounding Bay Area. My God, you have Alcatraz. Remember the movie *The Rock*, with one of my favorite actors, Sean Connery. Great movie, but also a high-worth target. You have how many bridges? Especially the Golden

Gate. There's the Hoover Dam; no, wait, that's in Nevada," he said focusing on that state's agent representative. "There's all your airports, amusements parks, and your I energy systems, although PG&E already has a lot of problems. What we (pointing to the other groups along the walls) are hoping you can do is to go back to your states and talk it up with your fellow law enforcement partners, and frankly--think as a terrorist. What targets do you think bin Laden would have loved to hit if the son-of-a-bitch were still alive. Where would he get the biggest bang for his buck and the most publicity? Osama was an egomaniac. He videotaped Fox News and the other talking head shows when they were discussing him, his whereabouts, or his future plans. We wish we could give you more specifics, but we have none. We don't know the *where*. We don't know *how many* jihadists. We don't know the *time*. Chatter continues to mention the month of March, but that month has thirty-one days."

Their group was dismissed at 2:15. Jeannie had the beginning of a massive headache trying to list in her head the number of high-worth targets, just in the city of San Francisco alone, much less the rest of the Bay Area. And then there was Agent Rich Pinheiro. She was the only agent he called by first name. "Don't flatter yourself girl; he probably has a woman in every state," she thought.

CHAPTER TWENTY-SEVEN

Jeannie did not look at the binder while waiting for her flight, nor while in the air heading to SFO. Instead, she secured it in her overhead luggage and continued listening to her audiobook. But, as she listened to the narrator tell the story, her mind visualized all the possible targets in her area that might fit the bill for shock-value if she were bin Laden. There were so many iconic landmarks in the city: from the Golden Gate Bridge, to Coit Tower, to the Palace of Fine Arts. And let's not forget the Bay-to-Breakers run. "When is that held?" she asked herself.

Recently, the tourist trade and convention bookings in San Francisco had declined due to filth on the streets, panhandling, and a liberal district attorney who seemed to not want to prosecute anyone. There were over 55 car burglaries committed a day in the city, and if anyone called for cops, the police often did not respond. But, with that said, there were still many conventions being held each month.

And what if the target were not San Francisco? Each of the surrounding cities boast attractions that terrorists might consider worthy to of attack and destruction. Santa Clara has a large amusement park located next door to Levi's stadium. There is the boardwalk in Santa Cruz, and there are many churches, synagogues, and places of non-Islam faith. "Oh well, she thought, I'll take the information to Lomax and together we'll come up with a plan for how to proceed," she told herself as she tried to get back into the book. "I wonder if I 'll ever run into Agent Pinheiro again?"

Tami, Jeannie's secretary, picked her up at the airport. Ismail was in court working on an old case and was unavailable. She attempted to bring Jeannie up to speed on what had transpired in the office during her trip to D.C., but Jeannie could not concentrate.

"Is the SAC in his office today?" Jeannie asked.

"Yes, I saw him arrive around 7:45. He has a light schedule today, so I'm sure you can go in and see him," Tami answered.

"Good," Jeannie replied. "Our entire office will be occupied with what was laid on me at Quantico. Do you know when the Bay-to-Breakers run is scheduled?" she asked Tami.

"I think it's in either May or June, but I'm not sure," she replied.

"That's good," Jeannie said, which puzzled Tami.

Jeannie and Tami were back at the bureau garage the same time Ismail returned from court. He looked pissed, but when he saw Jeannie he smiled and walked over to her car and took her luggage from her. "You know, this is why men die sooner than ladies," he said.

"And why is that, my scholarly friend?" Jeannie asked.

"Man, we have to carry luggage, push the shopping cart, take out the garbage, wash the car, open doors for you ladies. It takes a toll, you know."

"Oh, give us a break. You macho males love it," Jeannie replied as Tami nodded her head in agreement.

"So Boss, how was your visit to the swamp?" Ismail asked.

Jeannie told Ismail and Tami what she had learned in D.C. When they arrived at their floor, Jeannie opened her carryon bag, took out the binder and handed it to Tami, asking her to make two additional copies, one for Lomax and one for Ismail.

"Gee, from the size of the binder, that's a lot of potential targets," Ismail said.

"You don't know the half of it," Jeannie responded. "I have never seen that many agents from the FBI, ATF, NSA and Homeland Security together at one time. There weren't that many after the Boston Marathon bombing. We definitely have our work cut out for us, and I will brief you and the team once I meet with the SAC."

Lomax waved Jeannie into his office while he was ending a phone call. After hanging up, he asked her how the trip was and other mundane questions. There was a knock on his door frame and they both saw Tami with three binders in her hands. Jeannie stood and took them from her and handed one to Lomax. He briefly thumbed through it as Jeannie shared the essence of the Quantico briefing.

"So, the NSA and DHS think that bin Laden may strike from the depths, huh?" he asked.

"They're basing this on the increase in chatter and frequent reference to the month of March. I got a headache after the meeting, trying to sort through the overwhelming number of possible targets we have in the Bay Area. Frankly, I hope your experience in Counter-Intelligence will help me form a plan on how to proceed." With this Jeannie waited for his response.

Lomax did not immediately respond. He glanced at the binder contents for a few seconds and then looked at Jeannie. "First, you have to understand that there is no way in hell we can secure every possible target in our area from terrorists. Look at all the time the terrorists took to prepare for the 9-11 events. We have two months. For all we know, al Qaeda may already have terrorists in position for an attack. Alright, let's get all hands on deck. Get everyone in here for a briefing at 9:00 a.m. tomorrow--no exceptions unless they have court or something that can't go on the back burner. Have Tami make up enough binders for everyone that will be present. In the meantime, you and your team should go over this list and try to prioritize what's in the city, and then farm out everything we can to the rest of the Bay Area law enforcement community. The name of the game is 'cover-our-asses.' We don't want these assholes to hit us, and later have some investigative reporter finds out that we had information on a target and never shared it. I'll do the same, and also make a few calls to my former colleagues in arms to see if I can pick their brains."

"Jesus Christ! I can name over twenty-five sites just from the first page of the binder," Ismail said as Jeannie entered her office and saw him sitting in a chair across from her desk.

"What did the SAC say?" he asked.

"Basically, what you said. There is no way we can possibly cover all of these main targets. Somehow, we need to prioritize the most likely targets, thinking as bin Laden," she replied.

"OK, so now I can play camel jockey and decide what I'd like to see blown up," he said while laughing. "Just call me Mohammed. I'll get back to you after lunch. Do you want the rest of the team to be briefed, or do you want to wait until tomorrow morning for the all-hands-on-deck meeting?"

"You know, I'd like to get our team together today. Contact everyone, and see if Darcy is free. Her analytical mind will be a definite asset. Where are you going for lunch?" Jeannie asked.

At 1300 hours the entire team was in the smaller of the two briefing rooms. Tami had already printed enough binders for the meeting to give Jeannie's team a binder the day before.

Jeannie provided a brief narrative of what she learned in Quantico, and had them take several minutes to peruse the binder contents. She could hear rumblings from her agents, many of whom shook their heads as they went through the columns of potential targets. At approximately 1315 hours she called for their attention and told everyone to think like a terrorist, specifically the former leader of al Qaeda, and what sites came to their mind. She had Darcy write several of the "targets" on a whiteboard as they shared ideas. Jeannie thought to herself that she was missing something, but she could not put her finger on it. Hopefully it would come to her in time.

By 1500 hours, everyone was starting to go rummy, so Jeannie ordered-in several large pizzas and drinks for her team. "Can't think on an empty stomach," she thought. Everyone

dug-in when the pizzas arrived. She could sense frustration in her team members as they ate. "OK, everyone. It's 1600 hours. Everyone can go home early since you have to double back by 0900 tomorrow, and please don't be late for the SAC." Darcy said she wanted to put in a few more hours, correlating the information and ideas the group proposed so she could give them a synopsis in the morning. She would take the last BART train from the city to Hayward.

After stopping for a few groceries, Jeannie parked her vehicle in the garage and walked into her kitchen from the garage door entrance. She would tend to her mail sometime the next day if she remembered. She popped a frozen Stouffers turkey tetrazzini dinner into the oven--she was addicted to them--and turned on the television as she opened a can of diet ginger ale. As she stripped out of her bureau clothes and donned her favorite black sweatpants and Giants t-shirt, she heard two talking heads on Fox News discussing the simultaneous arrival on March 10th of the United States president and the pope. “Oh shit!” she said out loud to herself. “Talk about two major targets that bin Laden would love. They have to be placed at the top of the chart!” She immediately called Lomax and Ismail.

CHAPTER TWENTY-EIGHT

Jeannie couldn't sleep: thinking about the president's fundraising rallies well as the pope's visit. She was up several hours searching the Internet for the times and dates of the two events. With the president's fundraising event scheduled at the Cow Palace in Daly City and the pope's meeting with members of the Russian Orthodox Church in San Francisco, both taking place on the night on March 10th, she began calculating the manpower that would be needed. The Secret Service would call the shots for the president's rally, but security for the pope's visit would fall on both the San Francisco PD and the FBI, and probably on many other law enforcement agencies as well.

Jeannie arrived at the bureau at 7:00 a.m. the following morning, and she and Tami went to a nearby donut shop to purchase finger-food for the attendees. Darcy said she would get the coffee and hot water ready when she got in. Tami had placed binder copies on the floor near the side wall upfront near the small podium in the largest of the briefing rooms. Ample table space had been provided for agents to review the binder contents while they ate and drank.

By 0850 hours, most of the tables were occupied by agents of the entire San Francisco bureau. Jeannie's team was seated at the front table. Ismail stood and quickly walked to the main entrance door as if he had seen a long-lost friend, nodding at the SAC as he passed. Jeannie saw him wrap his arms around a male who, to her surprise, was Agent Pinheiro. "Well, oh well," she thought. While Ismail was talking to Pinheiro, Jeannie saw NSA agent Fahima Saban enter, appearing as striking as she was on the stage in Quantico. Her long shimmering black hair easily reaching the small of her back, her Middle Eastern features turned most of the male agents' heads. As Lomax walked towards the podium, Ismail who had been walking with Pinheiro, approached Jeannie who was standing near the wall with the binders.

"Jeannie Loomis. It's so nice to see you again," Pinheiro said as he extended his hand.

"You two know each other?" Ismail asked.

While shaking Jeannie's hand, Pinheiro said they met at the meeting in D.C. "How was your flight home?" he asked, not releasing her hand.

Jeannie felt herself blush and said the flight was uneventful, and that she did not know the NSA and DHS would be here today. Pinheiro finally released her hand--which Jeannie was sure must have felt like putty. "So, how do you know Ismail?" she asked.

"This old Portagee? Hell, we've known each other for what, 15 years?" Pinheiro asked of Ismail.

"Fifteen years? We've known each other all our lives; we're first cousins," Ismail said.

"Our dads used to go fishing together, taking the whole family. My mom and his mom would set up camp, brew coffee, make linguica sandwiches with Portuguese red beans, and warm up some malasadas. We competed to see who would catch the most fish, and this Portagee would cheat," Ismail said, bumping deliberately into Pinheiro. "He'd promise to give money to any of his sisters who caught a fish, and then he'd re-hook them on his fishing pole and claim he'd caught another one."

"Where's your proof? We in the Department of Homeland Security, must provide proof," said Pinheiro in response.

"Proof my ass! God, you're looking good for an old man," Ismail commented.

"Old man? I'm a year younger than you," said Pinheiro.

"Good information. I know Ismail's age, so that makes Pinheiro three years older than me," Jeannie thought as Lomax asked for everyone to be seated--which everyone did except Jeannie and Tami.

"Ladies and gentlemen, I've invited our colleagues from the National Security Agency and Homeland

Security who flew in early this morning to help with the massive task that's before us. As you may know, Assistant SAC Loomis just returned from a meeting at Quantico where she was briefed on a possible terrorist act in March. We don't know the location of the planned attack, but the date appears to be March 10th. Before I say more about your assignments, I want to invite NSA Agent Fahima Saban and Homeland Security Agent Rich Pinheiro to introduce themselves, and give you a little more detail regarding this investigation." Lomax turned to both agents. Saban would speak first.

"Huh! I wonder if old Pinheiro has a thing going on with Fahima. They'd make a nice-looking couple," Jeannie thought.

Saban gave a shorter version of the D.C. presentation, primarily stating that the increased chatter gives the reality of a major attack credibility. Pinheiro followed her lead and discussed the al Qaeda terror timeline, emphasizing the two big events that Jeannie had given to Lomax. "On March 10th the president will be attending a fundraiser at the Cow Palace in Daly City. Conservative estimates are that there will be in excess of 50,000 supporters attending. The secret service will provide security for the president and the first lady, but outside the building, security rests with the Daly City PD, the South San Francisco PD, and the SFPD, to name a few. The Secret Service believes their security inside the Palace will suffice, but our concern is with the overflow crowd that will watch the event from outside on large projection screens. If that's not a big enough headache, protesters including Antifa are expected to try and infuriate onlookers in the hope of gaining some negative press. Now, in addition to the presidential fundraiser, we have the pope attending a meeting at Holy Virgin Cathedral in the Richmond district of your city. Although the pontiff travels with a small security team, they can't both handle the major event inside the Cathedral and the crowd outside.

We asked agents from various major FBI bureaus of each state to attend our meeting in Quantico. I see that Assistant SAC Loomis made copies of the binder she received at that meeting, which when you review the material, shows that although we feel these two events could be number one targets for al Qaeda in the San Francisco area, we can't dismiss other possibilities." With that statement, he turned and walked away from the microphone while Lomax approached it.

"OK, with that, maybe we should hand out the binders," he said, looking at Tami and Jeannie. Several of Jeannie's team got up to help, as well as Pinheiro who made a bee-line to Jeannie's location.

"Here, let me take a few and help," he said while staring deeply into Jeannie's eyes. She could feel the blushing coming on, and just said, "Thanks." "Hey, Flo and I are going out for a few beers after today's briefing. Would you like to come?" He asked. Although Jeannie wanted to leap into his arms and say, "Yes, yes, yes!" she subdued herself and said that unfortunately, she needed to take care of a few things at home.

He continued, "OK, I'm sure I'll be returning just before March 1st. Maybe we can get together for dinner then. What do you say?"

"I'd like that. Let me know a few days before you arrive" Jeannie answered, and realized that during this short conversation neither she nor Pinheiro had handed out binders. Of course, Ismail saw the entire interchange and would capitalize on it by ribbing Jeannie for a very long time.

Crossing the Dumbarton Bridge, Jeannie found herself focusing more on Agent Pinheiro, or as Ismail called him, "Ricky." He was obviously hitting on her, but in a nice professional way. "Got to be cautious girl," she told herself. "This guy might be like the guy in the song by Ricky Nelson, *Travelin' Man,* from the early 1960's. How do those lyrics go?" She began to sing to herself as she maneuvered her Vette through heavier than usual traffic.

I'm a travelin' man and I've made a lot of stops
All over the world
And in every part I own the heart
Of at least one lovely girl

"And this Fahima; she's drop-dead gorgeous. You mean there's no spark between 'Ricky' and this Middle Eastern beauty?" Jeannie wondered. "Come on girl, focus!" And with that she turned on her car radio and tuned in to a sports talk show where the hosts were talking about the S.F. Giants season being a rebuild project.

As instructed, Basem arrived at the mosque near San Jose at 10:00 a.m. He was escorted to the back of the building by the Muezzin, the person who calls for daily prayer. There, he met with a person named Fahid Dada. Dada extended his hand to Basem, and while shaking it asked, "My brother, are you, Sami, and Khalil settled into your motel?"

"Yes. Everything so far is going well, my brother," Basem replied.

"Good, good," Dada said as he motioned to the Muezzin who had remained in the room to bring the items from the closet. Upon his return, he gave two large backpacks to Dada and then left the room. Dada opened one of the packs and pulled out a suicide belt weighing about 33 pounds. He held up the object before laying it across his lap and told Basem that it was the latest, most supplicated belt al Qaeda had produced thus far.

Dada continued, "The older explosive belts usually consisted of several cylinders filled with explosives, similar to several pipe bombs. But this version is equipped with explosive plates. The explosive is surrounded by a fragmentation jacket that produces the shrapnel responsible for most of the bomb's lethality, effectively making the jacket a crude, body-worn, Claymore mine that the United States has used on our brothers. Once the vest is detonated, the explosion resembles an omnidirectional shotgun blast. Hundreds of infidels will meet there death on March 10 due to you and your brothers actions that evening." Dada handed the two backpacks to Basem who bowed and left the mosque.

CHAPTER TWENTY-NINE

The first person Jeannie saw when she arrived at the bureau the next morning was Darcy. "How late did you work last night?" Jeannie asked.

"Oh, I got out of here in plenty of time to catch the last BART train to Tennyson Road, Hayward, exit. I live only a mile or so from the station, and it sure beats the hassle of fighting traffic that late at night. I took BART back here this morning, and I'll drive my car home this evening. I contacted Burk late yesterday afternoon and told him about the large amount of data pertaining to possible targets. We worked together until I went home, and we think we have a way of sorting through all this information dump."

"That's great. How is Burk?" Jeannie asked. He worked well with Darcy during the Star Chamber investigation, and was critically wounded during the incident that killed the SAC and nearly killed Jeannie. Burk was a typical computer nerd, but when she put

Burk and Darcy together on the Star Chamber case, things really took off.

"He's great" Darcy said. "He asks about you all the time. He would really like to work for you again over here in the city and asked me to keep an eye out for any pending transfers."

"You know, that would be a great idea. I'm going to put in an emergency transfer request and get him over here asap. Do you want to be the one to tell him, or should I?" Jeannie asked.

"Oh, I'm sure he would love to hear it coming from you. I'll wait an hour and then call him and act surprised. When do you think he might make it over here so we can really jump on the NSA data?"

Jeannie pulled out her iPhone and checked her phone contacts, then pressed the call number and awaited an answer. "Jeannie, how are you?" asked James Wilson, the acting SAC of the FBI Roseville satellite office.

"Good, Jim. And you?" Jeannie asked while staring at Darcy and motioning that she wished to get over the pleasantries. Following a few minutes of small talk, Jeannie turned the conversation over to the pending al Qaeda attack, which in turn lead into the request for Burk to be immediately reassigned to the San Francisco branch. Jeannie added that as soon as the paperwork made its way through the FBI bureaucracy, she would send a request to Jim, enabling the process to happen more quickly.

"Not a problem," Jim said. "I know he loved working for you. When do you want this to take place?"

"With March 10th approaching—fast! How about today?" she responded.

"I'll give him the word and he'll be on his way. Actually, maybe I should transfer you to his line and you can make it official. I'll check-in with him in about ten minutes, if that's OK with you?" Jim said.

"Great! Thanks Jim--and good luck at your end in trying to identify possible target sites," Jeannie said.

"You too. OK, I'm going to transfer you now," Jim said as Jeannie waited through a short period of silence on her cell.

"This is Burk, can I help you?" Burk asked when answering the phone.

"Yes. Why in the hell aren't you over here in San Francisco helping Darcy and me identify possible terrorist targets?" Jeannie asked, forcing herself to hold back laughter while winking at Darcy.

"Jeannie! How are you?" Burk asked.

"Fine, and from what Darcy told me this morning, you two have an idea of how to filter through all this shit so we can be a little more proactive."

"Yes. We worked on that last night, and I think if we…"

Jeannie cut him off by saying that she had put in an emergency transfer and had already cleared it with Burk's SAC. She wanted him in her office early that afternoon.

"Really?" he said.

"Yes," said Jeannie, "And I have a very anxious computer nerd over here who can't wait to start analyzing--or whatever it is you two do together. So, I suggest you pack your things, say your goodbyes, and get over here pronto."

"Yes Boss. I'll be on my way."

After shutting off her phone, Jeannie said, "All right. When he gets here, you two put together what you have and then track me down so we can review. In the meantime after I find Ismail, were going over to 1700 Montgomery and check in with our friends at Secret Service.

Alilta and Mustafa returned from a nearby CVS pharmacy, each carrying a bag. When they got back to the motel, Mustafa gave Anwar part of the contents from his bag. He handed him some throwaway razors, shaving crème, and a bottle of Old Spice aftershave lotion. There was also a small pair of manicure scissors.

Alilta's bag contained the same kind of razors and a women's shaving crème product. She had a waxing session set up for March 9th. She, like Mustafa and Anwar, knew the purpose of these items and put them in their respective bathrooms until the night before their sacrifice to Allah.

"What have you been up to this morning?" asked Jeannie of Ismail whom she ran into in the coffee room.

"Oh, I was in court with that liberal ass Judge Geraldine Cutter Rossburg. You know who appointed her to the bench don't' you? What a bitch."

"Yah, another Obama appointee. How did it go?" Jeannie asked, realizing that Judge Rossburg usually goes out of her way to side with defense attorneys, especially on search and seizure issues.

"I think she was a little intimidated when she saw a Fox News reporter in the audience. You know, they had a recent bit on her rules on--I forget whose program--but they ripped her a new asshole for her liberal interpretations of the Constitution. Anyway, she ruled in our favor and I think the defendant will now plead to a lessor."

Jeannie said, "I need you to come with me to the secret service office on Montgomery. I want to compare notes about the president's upcoming fundraiser at the Cow Palace. Then I'd like to swing by that Russian Orthodox Church where the pope will be."

"Oh, I thought you wanted to go the Orthodox Church and confess the lustful sins you had when you met Ricky," Ismail said, followed with a chuckle.

"Get out of here," Jeannie said. "But since you brought him up……"

They arrived at the secret service office and had to park several blocks down on Montgomery Street. The usual low-life populated the sidewalks and Ismail had to jump to miss a pile of shit on the sidewalk. "Shit! and I mean shit," Ismail said. "This city is becoming a third world country as I speak. Look at that, he said as they saw an African American male lying on his side with a needle sticking out of his arm. Jeannie announced her presence to the man and asked him if he was alright. He squinted, looked up at Jeannie and said, "Get the fuck out of here, bitch."

"He's alright. Let the piece of shit lie here and get some rays," said Ismail as the two continued their walk to 1700. The Secret Service building was located in the North Beach area of the city. Before the liberal Democrats took over city hall, this was one of the most beautiful parts of the city. Tourists used to head to Pier 39 for fun or to get tickets for an Alcatraz tour. Now, a tourist was just meat for aggressive panhandlers.

They entered the lobby and checked the directory, finding the Secret Service office in Suite 300. After making their way to the suite, Ismail pushed a buzzer located to the right of a heavy oak door. The buzzer also had a call box. Ismail tilted his head towards an overhead camera to the right of the door.

"Can I help you?" a female voice from the little black box asked.

Jeannie, who had been there several times before anticipated the question and held up her FBI badge to the camera. With that there was a buzz, indicating the locking mechanism had been released, allowing them to enter.

The female receptionist was very friendly and asked them who they wished to see. Not remembering who the current lead agent was at this office, Jeannie began by stating she was the Assistant SAC of the San Francisco office and would like to see whomever is in charge of the future presidential fundraiser event at the Cow Palace.

"Agent Loomis, how are you?" said a middle-aged man coming around the corner of the reception desk.

"Oh my God! Tom, I didn't know you were with the secret service," Jeannie said as she gave him a warm embrace.

"Five years now and counting. I saw that you nabbed those guys trying to tunnel under the Bank of America building," he said. Jeannie remembered when they worked together for a short time in the Los Angeles bureau office. She remembered Tom working with the secret service concerning a visit by then President Obama.

"Yes, that was us. This is Agent Ismail Flores. He had a big part to play in the tunneling investigation. Ismail, this is my old FBI partner, Tom Jenson."

The two shook hands and Jeannie asked, "What made you jump over to the secret service?"

"Well, working with them when Obama came to visit got me interested. I heard that you don't get bounced around as much as you do at the bureau, and with two future teenage daughters, I didn't want them to experience what I went through with all the military moves my dad put us through," Tom explained. "Come on back to my office. Do you two want some coffee? Tina, the receptionist just brewed a new batch."

Both Jeannie and Ismail accepted the offer, and after filling their cups they followed Tom to his office. Jeannie got the impression that Tom must have been working his way up the ladder: he was given a corner office with a view of the bay.

"Nice office," Ismail said.

"Yes, we call it a multi-million dollar view the way real estate prices are rising in this city," Tom replied. "So, what brings the FBI to the Secret Service. Let me guess: al Qaeda and the possibility of an attack on the president at the Cow Palace.

"You got it," said Jeannie. I attended the Quantico conference a few days ago where the NSA and DHS gave us more than enough possible targets in not only our city, but the whole country. We were asked to think like Osama bin Laden, and prioritize which of these thousands of sites he would like attacked if he were still alive."

Tom leaned forward on his desk, picked up his cup of coffee and after a gulp, put it down, saying, "Yes, since we fall under the Department of Homeland Security, we were the first to learn of the intelligence found on the unencrypted devices in the SEAL raid. Our office will be assisting the Protection Division prior and during the arrival of the president. He'll be staying at the Ritz-Carlton, but we feel that if they're planning an attack, it would be the Cow Palace location."

Tom kept some of the security measures close to the vest, especially regarding the security that would be in place by the Protection team. Declining another cup of coffee, Ismail shook hands with Tom, and after Jeannie gave him a hug, they left the building.

Alilta found a smaller box inside the backpack that contained the suicide vest. She placed the straps over her arms and put the "bump" over her stomach while looking in the bathroom mirror. She then placed a long-sleeved dark tee-shirt displaying a picture of the president and the slogan, *Four More Years* over her head. She was pleased that she looked like a lady in the final months of pregnancy. The killing of her husband by the Americans prevented her from actually carrying a child that might have been. Allah will get his revenge with her help.

CHAPTER THIRTY

"Good morning, Mr. President," the FLOTUS said while winking. "Do you have a busy schedule today?" she asked. The former model had entered the breakfast nook area in a white Armani pants suit. Her hair was long and wavy, just the way it was when she first met her husband, now president of the United States, for the first time. She knew her husband liked to eat right next to the kitchen so he could talk and joke with the kitchen staff. Paulie, the chief chef, was retired from the U.S. Navy and the president never stopped bragging about the great meals he put together, including a different type of breakfast strictly for the president each morning.

"No different than all the other days, my darling," the president responded. "How about you?"

"We will be meeting to discuss the Easter Day celebration on April 12th. Having done it for the last three years, I think we've got a handle on it. Other than that, I think I will take our son to the park and let him play with his new remote-controlled speed boat. He has grown attached with Agent Listrom, you know the tall secret service agent. I hope that after your re-election, we can build in some time for us to just get away, or at least out of Washington for a while. I absolutely hate it here. The left hates the right--the right hates the left."

The president stood and walked to the other side of the table and bent over to kiss her on the crown of her head. "We will, I promise. This swamp's a lot deeper than I even thought it was, but we're making progress and four more years will go a long way to making America a proud nation again." He left her as a kitchen worker brought fresh-squeezed orange juice and green tea. "See you tonight," he said as he headed to the Oval Office.

Upon entering the room, he was filled-in as to whom he would be meeting with throughout the day. First up were the heads of NSA and the DHS. Wilson Carter, representing the DHS was just north of the president's age, but where the president had a full head of hair, Carter was totally bald. He told the president after his appointment that he started shaving his head instead of trying to fool everyone with a hair-crossover. Carter had been a rear-admiral in the Navy and served for over 25 years. The president enjoyed his "cut to the chase" attitude when being briefed by his subordinates.

Sandi Scott was in her in her early forties, and if a person looked up “librarian” in an on-line search, there would be a picture of Sandi. Still wearing her hair in a 1980 fashion and wearing black oversized glasses, she was not a head turner. But what she lacked in beauty, she more than made up for in intelligence. She graduated the first of her class from MIT, and was very instrumental in helping the NSA and the CIA track down bin Laden’s courier, and later his compound.

“Good morning,” each one said as they entered the room, heading to the chairs they normally used during briefings. Each was carrying binders.

“Good morning, and what do you have for me today?” the president asked.

Scott went first, and establishing eye contact with Wilson said, “Sir, there’s been an uptick in traffic coming out of the Middle East regarding a pending attack on the United States.”

“How reliable is the information?” the president asked.

“We haven’t seen this much chatter since the days leading up to the 9-11 attacks sir,” she replied. The president looked at Wilson, giving him an opportunity to jump in, which he did.

“Mr. President, as you know, we are still working our way through the treasure trove of intelligence gathered from the raid on bin Laden’s compound. We (directing a hand gesture to Scott) have completed our investigation of the encrypted devices; and therefore, consider what we found priority items.

"Yes, I know," said the president. "That's how we were able to prevent that explosion on the Amtrak train in Baltimore. Good work by the way."

"Thank you, sir," Scott said, taking over the conversation. "We moved on to the undecrypted devices and have found bin Laden's personal diaries in which he listed several future targets both here and abroad." She stood and walked over to the front of the president's desk, giving him a binder identical to those they had carried in. "This is the most recent list we've complied from his journals. As you see, there are thousands of possible sites listed both here and in Europe, as well as Africa and Asia. But recent chatter keeps referring to March 10th, the date we feel something's going to happen." She paused as the president turned several pages in the binder. When he finished, he looked at both of them, giving them the choice of who should continue.

"Mr. President," Carter said, "We've disseminated this information throughout the law enforcement communities, and as we speak, they're working as diligently as they can to place priorities on various potential sites, but with only two months left, we, the NSA, and the DHS don't feel that every possible potential target can be checked out." With that, both Carter and Scott sat with their hands interlaced on their binders.

"I see," the president said. "And I suspect that you have your own ideas as to sites that would interest al Qaeda?"

Looking at each other, Carter said, "Yes sir. We feel that your planned fund-raising event in California fits all the criteria that would intrigue bin Laden if he were alive."

The president seemed to be lost in thought until he lifted his eyes from the contents of the binder in front of him and said, "Did either of you know that Lincoln had an interest in the predictive power of dreams? Abraham Lincoln's former law partner, I think his name was Ward Lamon, a friend and sometime bodyguard—told a famous story about the 16th U.S. president's premonition of his own death. According to the tale, just a few days before his assassination on April 14, 1865, Lincoln shared a recent dream with a small group that included his wife, Mary Todd, and Lamon. In it, he walked into the East Room of the White House to find a covered corpse guarded by soldiers and surrounded by a crowd of mourners. When Lincoln asked one of the soldiers who had died, the soldier replied, 'The president. He was killed by an assassin.' Interestingly, Lincoln supposedly later insisted to Lamon that the body on display was not his own—so he, himself did not view the dream as a portent of his own demise. No one is sure if the story is true or not. Even if Lamon's story isn't true, Abraham Lincoln was apparently quite interested in the meaning of dreams and what they say about future events, both positively and negatively. Truthful story or not, Lincoln didn't seem to feel he had a premonition of his own death. He once said that anyone determined to kill a man, could easily walk right up to a potential victim and shoot him. No one could stop it from happening.

Just look at what the Japanese did when they realized the war was being lost. Similar to al Qaeda, they recruited young men for their 'special attack units.' Nothing more than martyrdom. These pilots were men who were mentally prepared to die. All we can do regarding this information is to operate with due diligence which you and law enforcement are doing, but I will not give in to terrorism and cancel my event. I'm sure you two have briefed my secret service protection team, and I'll leave it in your and their hands."

CHAPTER THIRTY-ONE

Jeannie had Ismail drive to Holy Virgin Cathedral, the large Russian Orthodox Church located on 6210 Geary Boulevard. It is located in the Richmond district that has a large Russian population. Jeannie thought the church was gorgeous with its five onion domes covered with 24-carat gold leaf. She knew it was the largest Russian Orthodox Church in San Francisco, although she did not know its capacity.

"Are you planning to go inside?" Ismail asked.

"If you're implying I need to confess my sins, no; I'm not going inside," she said.

"Hey, don't jump down my throat. I'm not the one having sex dreams with Ricky," he said as Jeannie socked him on his right shoulder.

Jeannie got out of the car and Ismail followed. He watched her as she shaded her eyes while looking in both directions from the church. "Shit!" she said. "Geary has all these intersecting streets, and everything is so close together. SFPD is going to have their hands full if this is the target," she said as she continued to survey the area surrounding the cathedral.

"Hey, I'm hungry. What about checking out one of these Russian restaurants? They seem to be on every corner," Ismail said.

"My God, the Portagee wants to eat Russian food?" she asked.

"Hey, I was just thinking that when Ricky returns and you two hook-up, you can take him to a nice Russian place. I've got to look out for my cousin, you know," he said with a straight face.

"We're not hooking-up. He's coming to the city soon and he asked me if he could take me to dinner. I said yes. Just two professional law enforcement agents having a meal together," she said.

"Uh huh! That's why you turned bright red when he was talking to you, when you should have been giving out binders," came the quick response from Ismail.

"Lets' go, idiot," Jeannie said as they got in the car and started looking for a nice place to eat. They settled on a Russian Renaissance Restaurant on Geary Boulevard, just a few blocks from the church. The restaurant had approximately fifteen tables all sporting square white and blue tablecloths. In each of the white tablecloth squares was a picture of a famous Faberge egg that Carl Faberge presented to the Czar of Russia at Easter time. On the side walls there were various types of Matryoshka dolls, also known as Babushka dolls, stacking dolls, or nesting dolls. Some of the dolls were painted wearing traditional 1800s clothing, while others displayed famous celebrities and political figures from Lenin and Stalin, to Putin and President Trump. There where dolls of famous Russian composers, and replicas of the famous Faberge eggs themselves.

A male server came to the table and said, "Dobryy den," which Jeannie knew meant good afternoon. Jeannie replied with "Good afternoon" in English which told the server that Russian was not their primary language. "Please," he said as he gave each of them a menu.

Fortunately, it was written in both Russian and English and had accompanying pictures of the entrees.

"Shit, I don't know what to order," Ismail complained. I don't want a cooked dog or cat. You know, I heard that some Chinese restaurants do that."

"Please!" Jeannie said. "I'll order for both of us."

"How do you know so much about Russian food?" he asked.

"When I was a small girl, our neighbors for a short time were from Ukraine, but were born and raised in Russia. It was all part of Stalin's desire to place as many Russians as he could in occupied countries controlled by the Soviet Union. He knew that somewhere down the line the Soviets would be pushed back into their own country, but for the meantime he could force change on those occupied countries such as speaking Russian and adopting a Soviet style government.

Anyway, my mom would invite them over for dinner and they'd bring several authentic Russian dishes with them. My dad hated it, of course--you know the whole Cold War stuff. But for me, I loved hearing them speak in broken English, which they always apologized for when speaking. I got to taste varenniki--like a dumpling that's usually stuffed with cheese--mashed potatoes, cabbage, meat and hard-boiled eggs. There was also borscht, which is a beet soup. My dad initially said he didn't like it, but whenever he started to come down with a cold, he asked my mom to check with Vierra and see if she had any borscht soup to help him get rid of his cough." The server returned to take their order, which Jeannie gave him.

"And, what would you like to drink?" he asked. Ismail again deferred to Jeannie who said, "He'll have a diet coke with ice (she emphasized ice) and she requested green tea. "Very good," the waiter said as he retreated to the kitchen.

"Why did you have to say ice?" Ismail asked.

"I don't think I ever told you, but before joining the bureau right after college I visited Eastern Europe. I went to Poland, Belarus, Ukraine, and twice to Russia," Jeannie started to answer before being interrupted.

"I would've taken you for a person who'd want to visit Paris or Rome. Why Eastern Europe?" Ismail asked.

"My dad and I were history nuts. Well, I still am. I watch the History Channel probably more than anything else unless a Giants or 49ers game is on. Anyway, I was fascinated with the Russian Revolution, Rasputin, the last Czar and his family, their assassinations. This included a desire to visit the Nazi death camps in Poland. I actually went to the Auschwitz--including Treblinka--and Sorbibor death camps. That lead to further excursions into Belarus and Ukraine. Anyway, back to your question about making sure your coke comes with ice. I found during my travels that Russians don't use ice in their drinks--room temperature is fine. I also learned that when ordering a coffee I needed to request an American coffee; if not, I'd get this little, tiny, almost doll-like cup of expresso with a capital E."

Ismail asked many questions about Jeannie's visits to the death camps and the different cultures she experienced in Russia. Their food arrived while they were talking. The waiter placed a dish in front of Jeannie containing a large portion of varenniki with a side order of fresh sour cream, and another plate with several slices of dark Russian Rye bread. Jeannie had ordered beef stroganoff for Ismail.

"Smells good," he said, after the server left. "I wonder if they can make this with linguica or chorizo?"

"Gee, I can't take you anywhere," Jeannie said, as she watched Ismail stuff stroganoff into his mouth like he had not eaten in several days.

After he finished his meal and while Jeannie was finishing hers, Ismail turned in his seat, turning almost a full 360 degrees to look around the restaurant. "What are you doing?" Jeannie inquired.

"I don't think this place is romantic enough for you and Ricky to hook-up," he said with a straight face. "You need a place with low lights, maybe a fireplace--you know, romantic."

"You won't quit will you. Do I have to call your wife and have her muzzle you?" she asked, trying to suppress a laugh.

"Hey, I'm just trying to help you out, and I have to look out for my cousin, you know," came his response. "Besides, my wife would feel the same way since, you know, she used to have the hots for Ricky until she found me."

"Really?" Jeannie said. "You said he was your first cousin, yet you're a Flores?"

"Yeah, we're first cousins on my mother's side. She was a Pinheiro--full blooded Portuguese. We practically grew up together being so close in age and all. That all changed when Ricky got a sports scholarship to play football for the University of Notre Dame."

"Wow, impressive," Jeannie said.

"Ricky was great at football and I was pretty good with the bat; but for me, I never had delusions of making it to the "bigs." So instead, I focused on a BA degree and entered law enforcement. Ricky actually made the team with the Fighting Irish, only to blow out his knee two days before their first season game. He was already being scouted by the NFL as a freshman, but that all ended with the injury."

"OK, Ace. Since you won't let this go, tell me about Ricky--you know, everything a girl needs to know," Jeannie said, as the waiter removed their dishes and they waited for the bill.

"Well, if you really want to know," Ismail said leaning forward--but before he could say anything the waiter arrived with the bill. Jeannie picked it up, glanced at the amount due, added a tip, and they left.

Before reaching their vehicle where Jeannie wanted to continue the conversation about Ricky, her cellphone rang. Glancing at the screen she saw it was from Darcy. "Hi Darc, what's happening?" she said. Darcy told her that she and Burk were ready to show what they feel might help prioritize the various sites given to them by the NSA and DHS. "We'll be there in ten minutes, depending on the traffic from Geary Boulevard." It took almost 15-minutes due to an accident blocking both lanes of traffic. Jeannie took advantage of the time by asking Ismail to tell her more about Ricky.

"Gee, I think you've really got the hots for my cuz," Ismail said. Jeannie did not respond but gave him a look meaning, "Stop stalling." "OK, well after he was injured, he decided to stay at Notre Dame and finish his education. I think he majored in Political Science, but I could be wrong on that. He earned his Master's in the same field and had thoughts of attending law school, but when 9-11 happened he enlisted in the U.S. Marine Corp and became a Recon Marine. Being super competitive, he later left the Marines and became a Green Beret; you know, special forces and all."

"Green Beret? I thought they only existed during the Vietnam conflict. Did he see action?" Jeannie asked.

"Oh yeh," Ismail said. "He served three tours over in camel-jockey land and was honorably discharged as a decorated captain. The Navy SEALS get all the press nowadays, but the Green Beret are still very active and operate behind the lines, trying to convince the locals to stand up to the likes of al Qaeda or ISSIs. He thought about being a lifer, but got shot--believe it or not--in the same leg as the bad knee. His military career was over. He bummed around for a few years and we got together at a family reunion. We almost got into a fist fight because I got in his face and said he needed to stop feeling sorry for himself and get a job. That didn't go over well, and I took off. But the next day he showed up at my motel and thanked me for verbally kicking his ass. He got a job with the NSA with no sweat, but then switched over to Homeland Security because he felt that there was where the action is. What else do you want to know?" he asked.

"Is he married, or ever been married?" she asked.

"Ah, now we're getting down to the nitty-gritty, huh?" he said laughing. Jeannie just started at him as if she were pouting. "No, he has never been married--OK? That's what you really wanted to know. He's had a lot of girlfriends, but none were very serious since they didn't like that he was always deployed and was rarely around long enough for a serious relationship to develop. Before he volunteered to give out binders with you, I asked him if he was getting any, and he said 'no,' so you have a chance," Ismail said laughing so hard he drooled on himself. He wiped his chin and saw out of the corner of his eye that Jeannie's fist was headed towards his shoulder again.

"Gee, I may have to tell him that you might be prone to domestic violence. You know, I have to look out for my cousin's welfare."

Burk gave Ismail a big hug upon seeing him exit the elevator. He did the same with Jeannie, but with a little more respect. "Burk, welcome aboard," she said. "You're looking fit and trim. Are you ready to go to work?" she asked.

"You bet," he said, as the three of them walked down the hallway to Darcy's office where they found a large spreadsheet taped to one of the walls. Darcy got up and walked over to Burk, and the two of them began pointed to the listed items: Cruise ships, Disneyland, all the major sports arenas and sporting events like the Bay to Breakers, the Boston Marathon, major churches, military posts, cathedrals, airlines, dams, power plants and other infrastructures in all states, and all landmarks in Washington D.C. and other states. There were literally thousands of potential sites.

"Burk came up with an algorithm that we think will help us focus on sites with the greatest number of characteristics similar to previous al Qaeda targets, but pertaining solely to the San Francisco bay area. We'll share this algorithm with other states so they can do the same."

"Actually, Darcy had a lot to do with it," Burk offered, looking at Darcy who blushed at the flattery. "The algorithm places a value on each potential target, using the parameters that Osama bin Laden seemed to be leaning towards when he made his selections. The higher the score set by the algorithm, the more likely it is a target. This methodology was used for each of the fifty states." When Burk finished, he stared at Darcy who was again blushing.

Ismail cleared his voice, which turned the presentation back to Darcy. "Right. OK, well basically, using this algorithm we first calculated why we felt bin Laden chose previous sites, and then we computer sorted the sites given to us by the NSA, and this is what we got."

Jeannie and Ismail walked closer to the spreadsheet. "Wow," Jeannie said, noting that each of the fifty states had a ranking of potential targets as set by the algorithm. "And look what the two top priorities are," Jeannie said, pointing to the top of the sheet listing California sites.

CHAPTER THIRTY-TWO

Jeannie called Tami and asked if the SAC was in. He was, and Jeannie requested that he come down to Darcy's office. When he arrived, Jeannie introduced him to Burk, gave a short synopsis and history of them working together, and told of them both being shot and his technology expertise. Lomax welcomed him to the team and looked at the spreadsheet on the wall.

"So, what do we have?" he asked, staring at the sheet.

"Darcy and Burk created an algorithm based on past al Qaeda targets during bin Laden's regime. Using this last night, they came up with this prioritized list for our area," Jeannie said.

Lomax spent several minutes looking at the list, tracing points with his right finger. Then he walked over to Burk and Darcy and said, "Nice work. I would love for you two to show me how you came up with the algorithm. We weren't that sophisticated back when I was in Counter-Intelligence." Then, looking at Jeannie, he requested that she send a copy of the spreadsheet with a little background on how they came up with the algorithm, and send it to as many law enforcement agencies throughout the country as possible. "Next month is March. I guess I don't need to remind anyone, but the proverbial clock is ticking." With that statement, Lomax returned to his office.

"OK. Darcy, Burk; you heard what the SAC wants done. That falls on you two. Once completed, I want several copies that Ismail and I can distribute to Secret Service, SFPD, Daly City PD, and so forth. I know it's going to be a lot of work. I'm authorizing overtime, so get going. I'm sorry, Burk. You'll have a long first day here," she said, smiling.

"Not a problem," Burk said with a huge smile as he turned and looked at Darcy. "We'll probably need to condense the information and be brief since it'll be a nation-wide email. I don't think we need to discuss how we came up with the algorithm. Something like--here are the possible targets in your state prioritized by the FBI, NSA and DHS. What do you think?" he asked Darcy while Jeannie and Ismail left their office.

"I think we've got a little romance going on there," Ismail said.

"See, you guys all talked behind Burk's back that he was gay," Jeannie replied while deliberately bumping into Ismail.

"Yeah, who knew he was a skirt chaser. Way to go, Burk-man," he replied.

In Vatican City, the pope who is a very early riser, woke up before 5:00 a.m. per normal. He spent the next two hours praying, studying scripture, and getting the morning's homily prepared. He then celebrated mass, and of no surprise to his staff, ate pizza. Today would be no different than most others. Outside of public engagements, the pope's day-to-day schedule is essentially up to him: typically, more filled with appointments and prayers than rides in the Popemobile. He also chooses to live as humbly as possible.

The pope is also surprisingly modest as well. Traditionally, he resides in the grand papal apartment at the top of the Vatican's Apostolic Palace; however, he feels more comfortable in a two-room home in the Domus Santa Marta, a hotel-style building located behind a gas station. His neighbors include the cardinals who selected him during the conclave.

At 7:00 a.m. the pope headed down to celebrate mass in Santa Martha's chapel. As usual he was dressed down in a simple liturgical cloth. Rather than make a grand entrance with an entourage of altar boys, he chose to slip in from the side. Sébastien Maillard, the Vatican correspondent for Rome's *La Croix*, describes this semi-public event as "the most privileged way to watch and get close to [the pope]."

As usual, this day he framed his message with a "Thought of the day," and when he finished, he moved silently to the back of the chapel to pray among select attendees. As he prepared to leave, he personally greeted everyone gathered outside the chapel in the atrium.

He made his way to the hotel's cafeteria for breakfast--today he was on time at 8:00 a.m.—and occupied the table he habitually uses for breakfast, lunch, and dinner. He never dines alone. A few privileged guests where there to keep him company, while other visitors sat in the dining hall and tried not to obviously stare at him. The papal breakfast included freshly squeezed orange juice and membrillo (quince paste) – a popular dish from his homeland, Argentina--followed by the main course: various types of pizza.

Today he did not have a full schedule, only a half-day of official meet-and-greets, and then he returned to his second-floor Santa Marta residence. The entire floor had been appropriated to serve as a home office for him--the setting simple and austere. The workspace housing his desk is small, and the decor is restricted to religious objects. There, he busies himself by reading and reciting the rosary when he does not go to the Apostolic Palace to address formal audiences.

The pope likes to be in charge of his papal routine as much as possible. He decides who he sees, and for how long. Often, he books appointments himself over the phone. If he receives a letter he feels especially touched by, he will phone the sender directly. He often spends his Sundays corresponding with friends in Argentina, including those in prison whom he used to visit while living there.

It was now mid-afternoon, and since he had been up since sunrise (or before, depending on the time of year), he took his typical pause during the workday for an hour siesta. After awakening he picked up work again, hoping to devote the evening to correspondence.

The pope heard a knock at his door and granted entrance to Cardinal Bianci. "Your Holiness, I wanted to go over your travel schedule for next week if it is now convenient," he said.

"Yes, my trip to San Francisco. Sit down," the pope said.

"Your flight on Shepherd 1 will leave at 7 a.m. on March 8th, and you will stay over-night in Detroit at the Four Seasons hotel. You will have no events in Detroit, so you can rest for the second part of your trip on the morning of March 9th. You will stay at the St. Regis Hotel in San Francisco and then motorcade to the Holy Virgin Cathedral where events are scheduled to begin at 2:00 p.m. Do you want me to go over the agenda?" he asked.

"No, that will not be necessary. You and I will have plenty of time during our trip to review the subject matter. I just pray that this in not another hopeless exercise in trying to bring our two churches together," he said, returning to his correspondence as the Cardinal left.

The pope's eyes tired as he worked, so he removed his glasses and closed them tightly while rubbing them with his fingers. He then placed his right arm across his chest and held up his head with his left hand. He kept his eyes closed and wondered, thinking about the East-West Schism that occurred in 1054, although no one really knows the date when the schism actually started. It might have started as early as the Quartodeciman controversy at the time of Victor of Rome. Orthodox apologists point to this incident as an example of claims by Rome to papal primacy and its rejection by Eastern Churches. He hoped that in San Francisco they wouldn't get bogged down in discussions about how, where, or when it occurred. Instead he thought they should focus on what they have in common and go from there.

Traditional Orthodox teaching claims that "those who reject Christ will face punishment." According to the Confession of Dositheus, persons go immediately to joy in Christ or to the torments of punishment. In Orthodox doctrine there is no place without God. In eternity there is no hiding from God. In Catholic theology, God is present everywhere, not only by his power, but in himself. Hell is a state of self-selected separation from God.

Eastern theology considers the desire to sin a result of spiritual sickness (caused by Adam and Eve's pride), which needs to be cured. One such theologian gives his interpretation of Western theology as follows: "According to the holy Fathers of the Church, there is not an uncreated Paradise and a created Hell, as the Franco–Latin tradition teaches." The eastern Church believes that hell or eternal damnation and heaven exist and are the same place, which is being with God, and that the very same divine love (God's uncreated energies) which is a source of bliss and consolation for the righteous (because they love God, His love is heaven for them) is also a source of torment (or a "Lake of Fire") for sinners (because they don't love God, they will feel His love this way).

The Western Church speaks of heaven and hell as states of existence rather than places, while in Eastern Orthodoxy there is no hell per se; there is only damnation or punishment in eternity for the rejection of God's grace.

The Catholic doctrine of the Immaculate Conception which claims that God protected the Virgin Mary from original sin through no merit of her own, was dogmatically defined by Pope Pius IX in 1854. Instead, Orthodox theology proclaims that Mary was chosen to bear Christ, having first found the favor of God through her purity and obedience.

"All petty differences," the pope thought. "Why can't both sides start with the doctrines we share, and then go forward instead of splitting hairs over differences." He feared that this would again end in a stalemate.

CHAPTER THIRTY-THREE

The U. S. president and the pope arrived for the first leg of their respective journeys within two hours of each other. For the pope, it would be a brief stay in Detroit with no formal duties. For the president, he would "work" the selected extremely wealthy and powerful few who would have dinner with him at the Ritz-Carlton. Moving around the crowd with a glass of water in hand that looked like a vodka martini, he shook hands and exchanged kisses as appropriate. Neither the governor, mayor of San Francisco, or the state's two senators were in attendance, nor were they expected. The president had made many statements during his first term in office over the sad state of affairs California found itself in due to a Democratically controlled house.

Jeannie's phone rang and she could see it was Tami. "What's up, Tami?" Jeannie asked before Tami could say anything.

"Hi, I have an Agent Pinheiro from Homeland Security who wants to talk with you," Tami said with no hint that she felt a romance in the air.

"OK, thanks. Put him through," she replied as she felt her pulse rate increase.

"Agent Pinheiro, how are you?" Jeannie said.

"Please, call me Ricky," he responded, bringing a smile to Jeannie's face.

"When are you arriving?" she asked.

"Actually, I just landed at SFO and I'm waiting for my ride to the hotel. The chatter's really spiked, and I felt a need to be here on the west coast for March 10th, only three days away. So, I was wondering if you'd be free for dinner tomorrow night?"

"I'd would love that," she said, feeling her face turn red even though no one else was in the room. "Do you have a specific restaurant in mind with all your worldly travels?" she asked as flirtatious as she could.

"I don't know about worldly travels," he said laughing, "But since it is your city, maybe you can pick one," he responded.

"I know a few good places in the city," she said as sexually as she could. "What hotel are you staying at? I'll can pick you up tomorrow. What's a good time?"

They agreed that 6:30 p.m. would be a good time since some, but not all of the traffic gridlock would be out of the city by then--an important consideration when using the various Bay Area bridges. They no more than said goodbye when Jeannie went into panic mode. “What am I going to wear? Is it too late to get my hair done today? My nails will have to pass. Why am I so nervous? It’s only dinner for God sake,” she thought as she told Tami she had a headache and was going home early. She asked Tami to notify Agent Flores that he should contact her if anything came up during her absence.

The next day seemed to take forever to end. Jeannie, usually not a clock watcher, found herself doing exactly that. Her team had checked and rechecked with local law enforcement agencies to see if they had done their due diligence in checking out the algorithm priority lists of possible targets in their respectful jurisdictions. Now, it was time to wait and respond--something she hated to do.

Jeannie checked into a nearby motel and used the room and facilities to get ready for her meeting with Pinheiro--laughing at herself, knowing it was a date, not a meeting. She had plenty of time to shower, do her hair and get dressed. For the occasion, she wore a black velvet pants suit with a green silk blouse underneath to accent her eyes. Giving herself a twice-over in the mirror, she was satisfied with how she looked and headed towards Pinheiro’s hotel, avoiding the Ritz-Carlton area which had already become a nightmare for the SFPD. A huge crowd had formed outside the hotel that included hostile protesters and Antifa members.

SFPD officers were stuck between the proverbial rock and hard place. Most of the veteran force had left years ago when liberals began taking-over the city government, who then installed liberal law enforcement brass. From there, it went downhill quickly. Bragging about being one of the country's first sanctuary cities, these same left-wing politicians acted in shock over incidents such as the death of 32-year-old Kate Steinle who was shot by José Inez García Zárate, an illegal, while walking with her father and a friend along Pier 14 in the Embarcadero district--not to mention their refusal to work with ICE. So most young police officers put in their time, and then transfer to another agency to get out of the hellhole.

Driving up to the entrance of Pinheiro's hotel, Jeannie saw him standing outside waiting for her. She was stuck by how handsome he appeared wearing black slacks with a matching black cashmere over-the-head sweater. At first, he did not think the bright red Corvette could be hers, but after she rolled down the passenger window and asked him if he wanted a ride, he jumped at the opportunity. "Wow, the FBI must've gotten some government pay hikes I wasn't aware of," he said upon entering the sportscar. "Nice ride! I'll bet this baby can really fly, huh?"

"I've had it over eighty a few times," Jeannie said with a smile. "So, are you hungry?"

"Famished; and by the way, you look beautiful," he said looking at her, not focusing on the interior of the expensive Corvette nor the scenery they passed in route to the restaurant. "So, tell me about your car," he said.

"Well, after I lost my mom, I received my inheritance. My dad had passed years earlier. They both worked hard their whole lives to provide for me; you know, college and so on. They habitually put money aside for a rainy day, and also my dad was pretty good at selecting stocks. I really didn't know what their estate was worth until--well, you know, I lost them. With their investments and the equity in their home, I inherited a nice nest egg. I told myself that they never really got to enjoy what they had saved. That old saying, 'you can't take it with you' really applied to them. So, I told myself after I got shot that life is too short, and I'm going to fulfill some of my fantasies, within reason, and this is one of them," she said as she gestured to the car's interior.

"You got a lot of fantasies?" he asked with a big smile.

Jeannie started to laugh and said, "Gee, you're really like your cousin, aren't you?"

They arrived at the Uma Casa, a new Portuguese eatery located in the Noe Valley neighborhood. The valet opened Jeannie's car door and she told him the keys were in the ignition. He gave her a tag which she promptly placed in her purse. Pinheiro had walked from the passenger side of the Vette to meet-up with

Jeannie as she swung the gold chain of her purse over her left shoulder.

"Uma Casa," Pinheiro said. "A Portuguese restaurant. Wow!"

"Yes, your cousin and I heard about it, but we haven't had a chance to check it out. This'll be a first for me. I hope it's OK," she said as Pinheiro offered his arm as they climbed the stairs to the entrance.

"Smells great," he said, as he opened the door and allowed Jeannie to enter. They were overwhelmed with delicious aromas emanating from the kitchen. "Wow, it smells like my mom's house. I love it. You made a good choice," he said.

"If you only knew some of the bad choices I've made in my life," she thought to herself, as a waitress approached and asked how many were in their party. They were escorted to a table set for four. The waitress removed the two extra settings and placed them on a side table, then pulled out her order pad and asked what they would like from the bar.

Pinheiro ordered a Greygoose vodka martini with two olives. The waitress looked at Jeannie who said, "Do you have ginger ale?" The waitress said they did; and with their drink orders complete, handed them two menus before heading to the bar.

Without being questioned, Jeannie volunteered that she started having a problem with alcohol and had sworn it off. Pinheiro asked if it was because of her getting shot. She told him no, it developed a long time before that, but did not go into detail. Pinheiro felt that Jeannie was a little embarrassed, so he changed the subject after opening his menu.

"My God, this place has everything. Carne de Porco a Alentejana, Arroz de Mariscos, and even Bacalhau Gomes de Sa. Of course, my mother would try all of these entrees if she were still alive and say that hers was better," he said with a chuckle. He looked up to the ceiling and said, "Talking about you, Mom."

Pinheiro ordered the Bacalhau while Jeannie ordered the Arroz de Mariscos, an entrée of fresh fish, scallops, clams, shrimp, arborio rice, tomato-saffron broth, and parsley.

"I can't get over how similar your personality is to your cousin's," Jeannie said.

"Well, you know--yes, we're cousins--but he's actually more like a brother to me. We were practically raised together when we were small, living only a few blocks from each other. Those were the days when after you found out someone had chicken pox, you gathered up all your kids and took them over to get exposed."

"I remember that," Jeannie said. "Strange huh? Don't hear people doing that anymore."

"Our families got together for birthdays, baptisms, first communions, confirmations, and man did we have some awesome family reunions with the rest of the relatives. We went on fishing trips. We even bought a boat together, you know, both families, a big trailable cabin cruiser. But finally, as we got older, we both went off to different colleges, and well, the distances between us…… damn this is great Bacalhau," he said as he put another piece of cod in his mouth.

"Yes, I heard. University of Notre Dame. Correct?" Jeannie asked with a smile.

"Have you been doing a background check on me Agent Loomis?" he asked with a smile.

"Due diligence, that's all," she said, reaching for her ginger ale.

"Who's the narc? I know, my cousin, right?" he asked. Even though he knew where Jeannie got her information.

"I was pretty good at football and really thought I had a shot at the pros, but God had a different plan for me; and here I am, protecting the U.S. of A. What about you, Agent Loomis?" he asked.

"I'm afraid it's not as exciting as your life. I was born and raised here in the Bay Area. My dad was a cop for almost thirty-years before retiring, but then he died of a heart condition. With the help of my dad's old agency, my mom tried to file a worker's comp claim since everyone knew the stress of working the streets had eventually caught up with him; but the claim was denied and my mom didn't want to appeal. I went to college and graduated, but not to a university as impressive as Notre Dame," she said smiling at him, which he returned. "I continued college and earned a Master's, and was thinking of attending law school, but instead applied to the FBI."

"Ever been married? No kids?" he asked. By this time Jeannie knew it had become more of a date than just two colleagues going out to eat.

She took another sip of her drink and thought, "What the hell; he probably already knows anyway." "Yes, I was married two times, but no children." She watched for any facial reaction to her statement about being a two-time loser. Not registering any, she countered by asking him the same question.

"One time. No kids," he said matter-of-factly. "I could say it was all her fault, but that wouldn't be true. We married before I transferred to DHS. In the NSA, it was pretty much an eight to five job with weekends and holidays off. I mean, at the start there was shift work, but as I made my way up the promotional ladder it became a straight dayshift job. But I eventually got bored and transferred, and that's when we started having problems--the travel, the hours, always apart; it all took its toll. One night I came home unexpectedly and caught a man leaving the house, and it didn't take much to make the connection. She didn't deny it. Instead of allowing a blood-sucking divorce attorney to bleed us dry, we found a paralegal; and for $500 and a six-months wait, we were divorced." He paused and took a sip of his martini.

"Sorry," Jeannie said. "Do you two still keep in touch?" she asked, really not carrying for the answer one way or the other.

"Only for part of the first year. When it was time to file our income taxes it was better for us to file together. Beyond that, I haven't had any contact with her. I used to sometimes contact her mom and dad; I was really close to both of them. But over time, that ended too."

Jeannie felt obligated to give a little more personal information. "Well, as far as I know, neither of my former spouses cheated on me. The first marriage ended because both he and I were very career driven. Not much time for romance--our careers and advances totally consumed us. We woke up one morning and both of us laid our cards on the table, feeling that divorce was the way to go. The second marriage only lasted a few months. You know what they say about dating on the rebound. Well, I didn't listen to my friends who felt I started to date too soon after my divorce. Two weeks after the first marriage was finalized, I was saying, "I do" one more time. He had a hard time with my hours, training, travel--the whole FBI fraternity. To end that one--we, too, used a paralegal and separated the sheets."

They both ordered dessert after Pinheiro told Jeannie she had to try the Torta de coco, which was basically coconut pie. When Jeannie put a helping into her mouth, she could not believe how good it tasted, nor how many calories it contained! There was a moment of silence between the two as if they both were searching for something to say next. Finally, Pinheiro said, "I really had a nice time tonight Jeannie. Ismail was right. You're a very nice person, and if it's OK with you, I'd really like to see you the next time I'm back in San Francisco."

Jeannie decided to go for it by asking, "What about you and Fahima?"

"Fahima? Well yes, she's very attractive and smart as hell, but I like women--and well, so does she."

Jeannie wasn't prepared for the remark and could only say, "Oh." She grabbed the bill from the waiter and refused to allow Pinheiro to see the cost, nor accept any portion of the payment, saying "You can pay me back the next time you're in town." She felt herself glow while displaying a flirtatious smile.

She drove Pinheiro back to his hotel in silence--each trying to figure out how the night would end. As much as Jeannie would love to jump in bed with him, she fought the urge. They arrived at the hotel and Jeannie left the engine running while Pinheiro tried to find the door handle. "Tricky car to get out of," he said, and turning to Jeannie added, "Again, thank you for a great night. I want to give you a kiss, but for the life of me, I feel nervous. Jeannie released the shoulder-harness seatbelt and leaned towards him. He took the hint and did the same. The kiss was better than Jeannie had imagined.

"Please be careful tomorrow," Jeannie said, having no idea where Pinheiro would be.

"You do the same," he said. "Let's hope it's a false alarm." With that, he closed the door and waved to Jeannie as she pulled away from the hotel entrance.

MARCH 9TH

At sunset, Alilta unfolded her prayer rug and said her evening prayers. Mustafa, who shared a room with her, did the same. Finishing her prayers, she was the first to use the bathroom around 8:00 p.m., carrying a small toiletry bag containing the items she purchased from the drug store. She first showered, and then sat on the fiberglass tub's seat which was now warm. She placed lubrication lotion on her legs and arms, and using the BIC razors, began the long process of removing as much body hair as possible to be presentable to Allah. Her pubic region was still sore from the waxing she had earlier in the day, and she could not imagine western women doing such a thing every summer just to wear a bikini that was offensive to God. The last thing she did was spray perfume over her body.

The three had been instructed to bathe and wear clean new clothes that would blend in with the crowd, avoid suspicion, and ensure uninterrupted access to the target location. It was Alilta's own idea, cleared by the mosque, to pretend that she was pregnant. She had purchased a cheap biker's helmet and placed a cloth around it to make it easy to attach to her under garments and form a protruded belly.

When she was done in the bathroom, Mustafa entered it and did the same thing, taking a little longer due to his thick chest hair. With care he trimmed his pubic hair and cut the hair on his head as close as possible, but he did not shave it. He then splashed Old Spice on his face and body.

Anwar performed the same ritual in his apartment. While doing so he remembered his instructors telling stories of past suicide bombers who had appeared in their dreams, saying they were now in paradise. He was also shown videos of previous bombers planning their operations. He, as well as Alilta and Mustafa had been radicalized to such an extent that they competed for the opportunity to launch an attack. He was there when Alilta, still grieving the loss of her husband, persistently asked the Amir to give her the opportunity as soon as possible.

After being selected, Alilita, Anwar, and Mustafa were told by their trainers that a suicide bomber wins paradise in exchange for giving up their life for Allah, and enters the afterlife the moment the explosives detonate. Once in paradise, the suicide bomber has the opportunity to recommend 70 people for paradise and Allah honors that recommendation. The bombers are told they are superior to other jihadists because they have no worldly ambitions such as status, money and esteem. While other jihadists can survive an attack on the enemy, the fidai (suicide bomber) faces certain death--the supreme sacrifice for Allah. As a result, there is a sense of pride among the bombers as they refer to non-suicide bombers as "common mujahids," and they are not allowed to interact or socialize with them.

Normally, before an attack is executed, only the top echelon of al Qaeda, the head of the training camp, the rahbar (guide) and the fidai know the target. But in this case, it was decided that the terrorist teams, now in positions to strike, needed to conduct more surveillance than normal due to the nature of their targets and to maximize the lethality of their mission.

They had been told that many suicide bombers leave behind notes that are delivered to their families upon their deaths. But now, with Anwar in the same apartment with Alilta and Mustafa, they decided to each record their "video wills" before their departure, which al Qaeda would release after their mission was accomplished. Mustafa and Anwar had also decided to visit their families for one final meeting before departing on their mission in the United States.

They planned to be driven to the cathedral together at 1:00 p.m., placing them in the celebration area around 1:30 p.m. The cathedral would have already been filled to capacity, and the overflow would have begun to swell into the street. When they arrived, they had the driver stop several blocks away once traffic had slowed to a crawl. Anwar paid the driver and the three got out of the taxi. Mustafa was wearing a shirt displaying the face of the pope giving a homily in Vatican Square. Alilta wore a similar shirt, but it was obvious she was well into pregnancy. Anwar walked away from the other two, carrying a Nikon camera hung from his neck. He was wearing a blue windbreaker with the word "Press" in yellow on both the back and front. Also hanging from his neck was a lanyard with several names of prominent media outlets.

The crowd already assembled was massive. Starting at the cathedral entrance, the crowd seemed to grow increasingly wider as it extended down both sides of the street. The three heard yelling and protests across the street from the main crowd. Many in this group held signs expressing hatred for Christianity, the pope, and religion in general.

Getting progressively closer to the center of the crowd, each of the three began reciting Qur'anic verses. The suicide vests worn under their garments appeared to be properly concealed. Even under the watchful eyes of many uniformed and presumed plainclothes police officers, they continued towards the center of the mass, avoiding contact with officers having a dog.

The orange color detonation cord connected their explosives vest to the striker sleeve, and was adhered to each of their left-hand wrists with duct tape. When they reached their respective targets, the ring of the striker sleeve would be pulled with the right hand and the blast would occur: they would enter paradise.

CHAPTER THIRTY-FOUR

At 2:15 p.m., the pope approached the podium to make his presentation and share his recommendations for ending the Schism. The church was packed to capacity with those who contributed the largest donations to the Russian Orthodox Church. Behind the pope sat His Eminence, the Most Holy Archbishop of San Francisco and Western America. A position not quite as high as the pope, but in the Russian Orthodox Church, a position near the top.

"Brothers and sisters in Christ," he said--just as a massive explosion was heard, causing many of the cathedral's glass windows to violently shatter, raining down on the parishioners inside the church. In addition to the screams and confusion within the cathedral, a whooshing sound passed through the structure. Although some people were crying, no one initially panicked.

Finally, some of the attendees began to leave the church as the pope and the Russian Archbishop were hurriedly escorted out of the altar area by the pope's security team. Those who left the confines of the church were not prepared for what they saw. Those injured had compound fractures, burns, lacerations, blast injuries, neck injuries, and some severe head injuries. There was blood and flesh on the walls of the church and neighboring houses. The smell of burning flesh and the taste of metal permeated the air, and blaring car horns activated by the blast dominated the noise. Some young police officers wandered around in a daze, waiting for someone to tell them what to do. But strangely, there was no panic. Then, second and third blasts occurred almost simultaneously. At that juncture, panic set in. Strangers were on the ground holding other's hands--telling them to hold on, that the ambulances were coming, that they could hear sirens, and that help would be there shortly. Additional senior police started to appear. When the paramedics and fire personnel arrived, they began a triage of the injured, determining the order of treatment for such a large number of injured or casualties, and assessing the degree of urgency needed to address various wounds. There was even a stronger taste of metal in the air and more smoke following the second and third blasts. Some described the smell as being similar to a barbecue, or a charcoal-like whiff of gunpowder mixed with blood and burned flesh.

A man was seen running in the street with his clothes on fire, with bystanders trying to put out the flames. Another man was missing his waist and legs--his upper body holding onto a speed limit sign. The blood was dripping and black. The impact of the three explosions created a path of destruction over 75-yards long. One small crater in the asphalt was created by Anwar. Alilta, and Mustafa were about one block behind Anwar when they set off their bombs within factions of a second of each other. They were so close to each other that they left a much larger crater than Anwar. Within 35 minutes, additional FBI agents and members of Homeland Security arrived, including Pinheiro.

Even after witnessing bombing in the Middle East as a Green Beret, Pinheiro was shocked at the amount of destruction he was witnessing. There were over 110 fatalities, and almost 200 were seriously wounded. Additional rescue workers and medical personnel were requested; but at best, it was organized chaos. An estimated 264 others were transported to local hospitals, some by ambulance, others by civilians using personal vehicles. The police under guidance of DHS Police closed off a 15-block area around the blast site. As the injured and dead were being identified, investigator found the precise street locations where the bombers stood when they detonated the bombs. Portions of their heads were found nearby, but nothing else. No one new whether DNA would help identify them.

Pinheiro issued a nationwide alert of what had happened in San Francisco to all state and federal law enforcement agencies. Secret Service notified the president who requested any and all updates as soon as information became available. Talking to the head of his protection team, the president said, "Well, now we know what the chatter was alluding to, and now we know the location. God have mercy of the souls of those afflicted." He instructed his speech writing team to modify the material he was going to use at his rally to include information about the massacre and his condolences.

While being driven back to his hotel under tight security, the pope asked his team to determine when it would be possible for him to make a statement, even thinking of returning to the scene of the destruction to offer prayer, and to comfort the injured and the grieving. He was respectfully, but quickly told that his plan would be out of the question.

Jeannie and the entire San Francisco FBI went into overdrive. Jeannie instructed her team to head to the site of the bombing. She and Ismail rode together. Lomax would remain at the office to act as the clearing house for incoming and outgoing information. Even with red lights and siren activated, Jeannie could only get her car eight-blocks from the scene due to the excessive number of vehicles and number of people running away, not to mention sick individuals holding their cellphone cameras and running to the scene. As they got closer to the actual bombing sites, the smell in the air almost caused Jeannie to vomit. Body parts, partially covered dead bodies, blood, smoke, debris, and blaring car alarms made it feel surreal. It was like the destruction she saw in the latest Rambo film, *Last Blood*.

Ismail spotted and pointed to his cousin who had just stood up after inspecting the crater left by Anwar. "There he is," he said to Jeannie. At first, Pinheiro did not see either Jeannie of Ismail. He was trying his best to decipher everything he was witnessing in order to issue proper commands, and to bring a semblance of order to the scene. Jeannie and Ismail worked their way through the wounded and dead to reach him.

"Well," he said. "Your team's algorithm nailed it. For the San Francisco area, it had this site or the Cow Palace as the top two targets that bin Laden would've loved to hit, and now from the depth of the ocean, the son-of-a-bitch strikes. God! So many dead. These bastards learned from the Boston Marathon, and this time they sent in three jihadists." He shook his head as if neither Ismail nor Jeannie were standing beside him.

"What would you like us to do?" asked Jeannie. Still in a daze, he did not respond initially.

"OK, SFPD has set up a perimeter and has kept most of the 'looky-loos' out of the area. If your staff could concentrate on finding evidence as to who the jihadists were, and then do the follow up investigation as to where they were staying…you know the drill." He said.

"We're on it," Jeannie said as she and Ismail walked around the first crater. She did not see Pinheiro briefly smile in response to her reply; she had already turned and begun work.

Basem told Sami and Khalil what he had just seen on Fox News. "Our brothers and sister stuck a dagger in the hearts of the infidels in San Francisco." "Allah be praised," they all said in unison. They turned up the volume on the TV in Khalil's room and watched as Fox's talking heads cautioned viewers that the following film clips would be graphic in nature. "We must honor our two brothers and sister tonight by carrying out an equally or better attack on those that attack Islam," he said.

Wearing latex gloves, Jeannie, Ismail, and later members of her team, began the long and arduous task of going through the rubble to collect evidence identification. They did not remove items of value, but simply placed numbered cards on crime scene items to gather later. During small-talk to break the tension, Ismail said he had learned from his time in the military of the motivations that prompt individuals to join suicide bomber training camps. He said, "Recruits are primarily motivated by atrocities against Muslims. The main theme in camp lectures is revenge. Their instructors call attention to the helplessness of Muslims whose daughters and sisters are dishonored by non-Muslims in Afghanistan and Iraq. These same camp leaders incite the audience when they narrate stories about Muslim women languishing in the prisons of infidels. According to camp instructors, innocent civilians killed in suicide attacks are martyrs, and therefore there is no need to be concerned about their fate." He looked at Jeannie who simply responded with, "Huh."

They found no form of identification for the three suicide bombers, only a lot of nails, ball bearings, and other forms of shrapnel that became missiles upon detonation. One of Jeannie's team members yelled and asked them to come to her location. The agent pointed to what was left of a fake baby bump. "Shit! The female apparently dressed as if she were pregnant," Jeannie said as she squatted next to the item and placed a number card on it. "Good job," she said while getting up. "Keep looking."

A second agent found the plastic remains of a lanyard with a picture of a male and what would turn out to be a false name. It also contained a list of network television names that was obviously used to trick law enforcement into thinking the bomber was a member of the media. There were hundreds of shirts showing the face of the pontiff, many stained with blood and splattered with human remains.

Jeannie tracked Pinheiro down and showed him the lanyard the crime scene team had processed and given to Jeannie for follow up. "We don't have anything to go by so far, and I don't think we'll get a hit on the DNA since they were probably all foreigners. What do you think about leaking out the photograph from the lanyard and seeing what pops?" she asked.

"Good idea. Maybe your SAC can hold a press conference and get that stated asap," he responded. With that, Pinherio continued to issue orders while Jeannie and Ismail headed back to headquarters. When they arrived, she gave an update to Lomax who immediately notified the press section to set up a press conference that would meet within the following hour.

Basem said, "Quiet," to Sami and Khalil, pointing to the TV. The Fox News channel showed a male's photo still visible on a badly burned lanyard. The anchor woman requested that anyone with information about the yet unknown individual contact the police as soon as possible. She said the police were listing the person as a "person of interest." "That must be one of our brothers who is now in paradise," Basem said. "This will work to our advantage. The police will spend all their energy and resources investigating our brothers' and sister's action today, giving us time to proceed with our plans. We should get ready. It is now our time to enter paradise."

CHAPTER THIRTY-FIVE

Jeannie and her team finished-up at the crime scene and returned to the bureau. Jeannie had told Pinheiro to contact her if he needed anything else. Pinheiro thanked her, but her feelings were a little hurt since he said it in a matter-of-fact manner with no romantic overtones. "Oh well," she thought, "Hell of a time to think about romance anyway. "

Over four hours had passed after the blasts when Jeannie and Ismail returned to the bureau. Jeannie smelled her clothes and they smelled of smoke and death, but there was work to do. She checked-in with Lomax who had completed the press conference several hours earlier. "Any new information?" he asked. "No," she said. We'll run the remains of the three jihadists, but unless they're already in the system, I don't think we'll get any hits."

An out-of-breath Tami appeared at Lomax's door. "Excuse me," she said. "There's a taxi driver on the phone who said he has information about the picture that was shown on the news." Jeannie glanced at Lomax, and without saying anything he quickly exited his office. She returned to her office and reached the male caller still on the line. "Hello, this is Assistant Special Agent in Charge Loomis. I understand you have some information about the photograph you saw on the news.

"Yes, I was on my break and I saw on Fox a picture of the same guy I dropped off at the Marina Inn over by Pier 39 several day ago. At least I think he's the same guy. He wasn't alone. If I remember correctly, there was also another man and a woman," he said.

Upon getting all pertinent information from the caller and concluding the call, Jeannie sent a team to his residence to show him the actual photo while she and Ismail drove to the Marina Inn. They met with the manager and showed him a copy of the lanyard picture. "That sure looks like the guy renting room 203. He has friends next door in 204--a male and a female. I think they're boyfriend and girlfriend," he said.

"Are they in now?" Ismail asked.

"I don't think so. They took off in a cab around noon or so," he answered. "Do you want to see their room?" he asked.

"Jeannie looked at Ismail and said, "What do you think? Still acting on exigent circumstances?"

"Hell yeah," Ismail responded. "If these three are the assholes that killed all those innocent people--fuck their constitutional rights. They asked the manager to first knock on the door to room 203 to see if anyone answered. Jeannie stood to the side of him with her gun drawn. Ismail kept watch for movement in room 204. Receiving no answer, the manager placed his pass key in the key slot and Jeannie heard the door click. "Hope this damn place isn't booby-trapped," she said to Ismail, at which time the manager moved several rooms away.

"Generally, not their M.O.," Ismail said.

Jeannie quickly threw open the door and took a shooter's stance while announcing she was with the FBI. Still no response. A quick look found the room empty. She then focused on room 204 and motioned the manager to return. Feeling only somewhat relieved from not being blown to pieces by a bobby-trap, the manager returned, and they repeated the action.

This room was equally vacant but appeared to have had two people staying in it. Ismail said he would conduct a quick search of 204, freeing Jeannie to return to 203. Knowing they needed a search warrant for both rooms, Jeannie called Tami and requested that she contact legal and get them started. She gave Tami the information the legal department would need to secure the warrants, and requested that once a judge signed off, several members of her team bring them to the motel.

Room 203 had a rolled-up prayer rug lying next to the unmade bed. "Bingo," Jeannie thought as she found numerous photographs of the Russian

Orthodox cathedral and its surrounding area. There was also a cellphone which she did not touch. She would let forensic go through it later. There was a disposable razor and shaving cream, and a bottle of aftershave lotion in the bathroom. On a table across from the TV were photocopies of various news agencies; some of the names had been cut out and were missing. Obviously, this is where he got the press credentials to put in the lanyard. She then went to room 204.

Ismail pointed at the evidence he had found. There were two prayer rugs next to the two twin beds. Both beds were unmade, so it appeared they did not sleep together. A female's blouse and man's shirt were on the beds. "They must have left them here and wore the t-shirts that were in this bag," Ismail said, pointing to a bag he found in the waste basket. It contained a receipt for two t-shirts, one male and one female. "In the bathroom I found two razors--BIC I think--some shaving crème, perfume and shaving lotion."

"Yeah, similar to what I found next door," Jeannie said. Just then, two San Francisco police officers arrived to secure the premises until agents arrived with the search warrants per Jeannie's request. The two officers went to the manager's office to announce that those two apartments were now considered crime scenes, and could not be cleaned until given the go-ahead by the FBI. The manager asked if these were the bombers in the attack? Jeannie told him it was too early to draw conclusions--although she and Ismail knew the answer.

Once Jeannie and Ismail were back at the bureau, Tami told Jeannie that the NSA had notified Pinheiro, who in turn forwarded the information to her regarding three positive identifications made by the agency. Facial recognition software identified the three suspected suicide bombers as Alilta Shammas, Mustafa Haddad, and Anwar Nafti. Photos showed their date and time of entry into the country.

Jeannie thanked Tami for the information, and then turned to Ismail saying, "You know, we have all this technology to identify these bad guys, but it seems as if it's always after the fact. What good does this do us now? What good does this give to the victims and those suffering their losses?" Ismail did not respond; he just nodded his head in agreement.

Wearing an oversized shirt displaying a picture of the president with the words, *Four More Years*, Basem left the other two. He would call Khalil when he arrived to report on conditions at the Cow Palace. Very little conversation took place between Basem and the taxi driver before he asked to be dropped off about six blocks from the main parking lot entrance. Wearing a baseball cap that said the same thing as his shirt, he felt he was blending-in with the crowd walking towards the complex. There were still almost two hours before the president would arrive. He saw a heavy police presence even that far out, but nothing he nor the other two did not expect. It did not take Basem long to see how the crowd would be funneled once inside the parking lot where at least ten jumbotron television screens had been erected.

A crowd of people about his age, carrying various pro-president slogans, began passing him on the sidewalk. With a smile on his face, he started chanting and joined the group. Approaching a checkpoint, he noted that the three officers standing there looked bored and nonchalant as the large group approached them. One officer's radio had drawn the officer's attention away from the group, and Basem used that distraction to gain entrance as if he had been cleared and was now waiting for his friends. "All clear," said one of the three officers, and the group, including Basem, reassembled and walked closer to the main auditorium.

Basem walked a short distance away from the boisterous group and called Khalil. "I am in my brother," he said. "The crowd here is very large and growing every minute." He told Khalil that he had waited for one of the police officers to be distracted and that was how he joined in with the chanting group of supporters, and that they should have no problem using the disguises they were given at the mosque. "Plan to be here by 6:00 p.m. when the president is supposed to take the stage and the parking lot around the large television screens will be filled with infidels." He hung up, and seeing a trash can placed the phone inside. Now he just needed to wait and let the victims come to him.

Jeannie's phone rang showing an unknown caller in her display window. "Hello, this is Agent Loomis," she said.

"Jeannie, it's Ricky. I just got a phone call from the NSA. Apparently, they've deciphered more ramblings from bin Laden's unsecured devices and he was contemplating hits on more than one target, similar to the four plane attacks on nine-eleven. I don't know if you were aware, but on 9-11 he had plans for similar plane attacks on the west coast. One of the intended hijackers was denied entry into the United States from Saudi Arabia, and bin Laden panicked and called those strikes off, allowing the attacks on New York to continue. The NSA feels that the President's fundraising event tonight and two targets in Los Angeles are the most likely ones to be attacked. I checked the algorithm listings and the two targets in LA look promising, so I'm heading to the airport with part of my team to be there by early evening. I wanted to let you know that the other half of my team will be at the Cow Palace. Do you have any resources that can aid us down there this evening?" he asked. Jeannie could hear airport noises in the background as he spoke.

"Not a problem," she said. "We'll head down there as soon as I hang up. Please be careful," she said, but he had already ended the call. She located Ismail and had him notify the rest of her team to meet in the smaller briefing room. While he was doing that, she checked-in with Lomax and told him what Pinheiro and the NSA had said. Once again, he would remain behind at the off-site command post while Jeannie and her team, plus other available agents, drove to the Cow Palace in Daly City.

"You know, this late in the game, the bombers could already be inside the building," Ismail said.

"I don't think so," Jeannie said. "Some of the more recent bombings done by ISSIs placed the bombers outside the most heavily guarded entrances. Look at the cathedral; they didn't attempt to get inside to take out the pope. They lingered around in the crowd, and when the numbers increased, they took that as a sign to detonate the bombs. The secret service protection team will have security as tight as a drum after what happened early today. No, if they're there, they'll be mixing with the crowd outside."

"Another thing," Ismail said before taking a pause. "These assholes can use two types of detonation triggers. One trigger requires the bomber to push down on the plugger that triggers the device. The other type of trigger is the worst kind. The bomber pushes down on the plugger, but it doesn't detonate the bomb until the thumb pushing it is lifted. If you could see the hand of a suicide bomber and see that the thumb is not pushing down, a shot to the head or the hand/arm of the suspect might prevent them from activating the device."

Ismail continued, "A shot into a suicide vest won't activate the explosives. Here's another problem. Most common security procedures with a suspected suicide bomber is to move the suspect at least 50 feet away from other people and ask them to remove their upper clothing in order to see if there is an explosive vest strapped to them. Most cops don't have a problem requesting this and it's relatively uncontroversial for use on males; however, it may cause an issue when dealing with female suspects. In training, a lot of male security personnel were reluctant to inspect females or strip-search them for fear of subsequent sexual harassment allegations."

"Well, aren't you full of good news this evening!" Jeannie commented while driving with the emergency lights on, but not the siren. "How do you know all this stuff?" she asked.

"Before I got picked-up by the bureau, I attended two bomb investigation classes offered by the LAPD, and Ricky has talked about bombs they discovered while he was in the Middle East."

Even in a bureau car with activated emergency lights and proper identification shown at several checkpoints, it seemed to take forever to reach the parking lot area of the Cow Palace where other emergency vehicles were parked. "My God, how many people are here?"

Jeannie asked of no one in particular. A uniformed officer overheard her question and said that the last he heard on one TV, was that there were over 36,000 in the parking lot and an additional 10,000 on the sidewalks leading into the area.

Jeannie thanked him and asked where the command post was? She and Ismail began walking towards it. The yelling and screaming progressively increased, and on the jumbotron they saw the vice-president approaching the podium inside the arena. "Look at that place. It's filled to the rafters," Ismail said. "If this is a target and they're inside, my God!" he said while shaking his head.

Fighting their way through the crowd, Jeannie's sixth sense kicked in. Something she had just seen or heard did not register right. She stopped moving forward and started taking a closer look at the crowd. Ismail proceeded about 10-feet before he noticed that Jeannie was not at his side. He turned and saw her intensely scanning the crowd. His sixth sense also kicked in.

Jeannie kept asking herself what it was that seemed out of place? "All of these people went through a metal detector, right?" she asked herself. "If so, who could have slipped through?" Before processing that question, she noticed two Middle Eastern males walking together; one was carrying a boom-mic secured to a pole while the other had a handheld microphone. They appeared to be wearing lanyards with media names. Her mind flashed back to the lanyard found at the crime scene in San Francisco, and then she noticed that both of their free hands had duct tape on them and that their thumbs were over a triggering device.

"Ismail!" Jeannie said. Ismail turned and looked at her. She had turned away from the two suspects. "Look behind me at those two males--one is carrying a boom mic and the other a handheld. Look at their hands and tell me what you think."

Ismail came over to Jeannie and placed his arms around her, as if to give her a kiss while focusing on the two individuals Jeannie mentioned. Ismail whispered in her right ear, "they have triggers, the type that needs to put pushed. We need to take them now."

Jeannie said, "When I count three, you take the boom mic and I'll take the handheld.

"Remember--head shots," Ismail said.

"One, two, three," Jeannie said as Ismail broke his embrace and stepped to the right of Jeannie. Jeannie spun counter to Ismail and they both pulled out their weapons. "FBI!" they both shouted. Before either of the two suicide bombers could react, they received headshots--spraying individuals behind them with blood and brain matter. Jeannie and Ismail shouted for everyone to move back, which was almost impossible in the huge crowd. Panic ensued by those closest to the actual shootings, but their screams seemed to be absorbed by the crowd's noise.

Jeannie checked the hand of her victim and removed the trigger device from the thumb of Sami Marek, and then cut the wires the way Ismail told her. He was in the process of doing the same thing with Khalil Qasim. “Ismail,” Jeannie shouted. “There might be a third suspect somewhere in the crowd.

“Yeah, but where?” Ismail asked as he turned around a couple of times, looking into the crowd of 30,000 plus. He glanced at one of the jumbotrons and saw the president of the United States approaching the podium, waving at the rambunctious supporters inside the Cow Palace who were unaware of what had just happened outside.

Police and federal agents were finally able to make it to the scene of the double shooting. They were told to request a bomb disposal team to the scene and to keep the crowd away until the area was contained.

Suddenly a shot rang out. Jeannie and Ismail detected a momentary flash from the roof of the Cow Palace. A sniper had taken a shot. At whom, they could not see from their vantage point. Then, simultaneously on all jumbotrons, a network camera crews’ video was being shown for all to see. A man dressed in a t-shirt supporting the president was lying on his back with most of his head missing. Numerous agents and uniformed police personnel responded to the scene of the third shooting that evening. Basem Tinazzi never knew what hit him, nor did he know he had been targeted by a member of the Homeland Securities sniper team.

Jeannie immediately notified Lomax and gave him the particulars, asking him to contact Pinheiro and give him an update. She told Lomax that both she and Ismail had given up their weapons to Homeland Security per protocol, and that they would be extremely delayed in responding back to the bureau due to having their statements taken and going through a general debriefing. Lomax understood, and upon completing the phone call told Tami to get representatives from the legal department and press release in his office as soon as possible, anticipating a press release.

Ismail and Jeannie drove to the office of Homeland Security. When they arrived, they were offered coffee which they both accepted. Two members of the FBI shooting review team arrived and told Jeannie that Lomax wanted them there during the investigation by DHS, so that if they came to the same conclusion, dual investigations would not be needed.

Interviewed separately, Ismail and Jeannie completed the interviews in less than two hours. Both compared notes on the way back to the bureau and sensed a clean shoot would be the conclusion.

Lomax had just wrapped up his second press briefing of the day and looked very tired when Jeannie and Ismail arrived. "Great job, you two!" he said upon seeing them. "Come in and sit down. Tami," he said into his intercom, "Please bring down cups and sodas for the three of us, and see if there's anything to eat in the breakroom--and if so, bring it down." He turned and looked at both Ismail and Jeannie saying, "You two look like shit, and I mean that in a complimentary way. When we wrap things up tonight, depending on how much time off the shooting board says you need, or if they assign you two to desk work--whatever, both of you will take a two-week R and R, and that's an order."

Ismail said, "Hell of a day, huh? I don't know about you, but I'm heading home to give my wife a treat, and then I'm going to sleep until tomorrow afternoon."

"I hope she tells you she has a headache," Jeannie said laughing. "Get a good night's sleep. You deserve it." Just then her cell phone rang, so instead of following Ismail out to the bureau garage, she headed back to her office.

"Jeannie, are you OK?" asked an out-of-breath Pinheiro. "Lomax called me about the same time my agents up there gave me the lowdown. Are you sure you're OK?" he asked again.

"Yes, I'm fine, and so's your cousin. Why are you so out-of-breath?" she asked.

"Oh, I'm running to catch a flight. It's a DHS plane, but they still get pissed off if we're late for takeoff. I'm flying back to San Francisco tonight to manage the ongoing two-event investigations. God, as it turned out, you got all the action. I wish the outcome at the cathedral had been the same as the president's fundraiser. Nothing happened down here in LA. Um, I hope, if we can find the time, that we can get together while I'm in San Francisco.... that's if you're still interested."

"Of course, I'm interested. The SAC has ordered your cousin and me to take two weeks off for rest and relaxation once we finish all of the damn reports, so I should be around. How long do you think it'll take to wrap everything up?" she asked.

"Hell, who knows? As you know, some things move fast. Facial recognition identified the three guys you got at the fundraiser. Once we learn where they were staying, we'll initiate search warrants, and so on. Then the work will really begin--trying to track down who sponsored them, their travel to the United States, and who their contacts were once they gained entrance. This president is like John Wayne; he'll not sit back and do nothing like Obama. Once he learns who sponsored this attack, that al Qaeda member or members will be toast. Uh--Oh, they're waving at me to run to the plane. I'll call you when I can find time. Thinking of you." The phone went dead before Jeannie could say she was thinking of him as well.

CHAPTER THIRTY-SIX

The DHS and FBI shooting review teams did not hesitate to rule that the shootings were clean, and they told Lomax that Ismail and Jeannie could return to full-duty assignment immediately if necessary. Lomax quickly notified Jeannie and Ismail of their clearance, but that they would need to secure a new weapon for a short time. Their weapons would remain with DHS for a few more days for forensic review, and then they would be returned.

He reminded both of them that they were to take two weeks off, but Jeannie told him that it would take several more days just for them to complete all the necessary paperwork about their part in the two bombing investigations and aftermath. As the weekend approached, Jeannie and Ismail told the SAC that they felt they could now take the offered two-week retreat.

Jeannie and Ismail were standing outside the open door to the SAC office. Lomax saw them, finished a conversation, and told them to take a seat. "This shit never ends," he said. "That was the NSA. They found a new fatwa bin Laden wanted carried out after his death, and another possible target they believe is again here in the city. They don't have time to decipher it and sent it to us. I told them to send it directly to Darcy because part of it appears to be in a code or riddle."

Jeannie and Ismail took the elevator to Burk and Darcy's new office. As they entered, Burk had just printed out the email and said, "Hi, it's in cipher." "What do you think?" he asked Darcy. "Cacsar cipher?" Jeannie looked at Ismail who returned the stare. "I think it is," said Darcy as she sat down and grabbed a yellow paper pad and pencil. "Let's see what we have here."

"Sorry guys," said Burk. "The Caesar cipher, also known as the shift cipher, is a great cipher that has a decent amount of security and is very simple. Before a person can start coding a message, they need to make a coder. You can make a coding wheel like what Darc is making on the pad. Looks good," he said to Darcy, who was showing Jeannie and Ismail what she had drawn.

"Here's how I made it, Darcy said. "I cut out a circle using construction paper or something. Then I write the alphabet along the outside edge of the circle so that it takes up the entire outside edge--see?" Not waiting for a response she continued to explain, "I then cut out another circle that's small enough to fit inside the first circle, making sure that none of the alphabet is covered up. I write the alphabet along the outside of the second circle so that it takes up the entire outside edge. That way that the letters on the second circle match up with the letters on the first. I then attach the second circle to the middle of the first circle with one of those pins you push through paper and then flatten the two ends so that it stays in place--like this one.

Now I have a coding wheel. A person just needs practice to know how to use it. First, spin the middle wheel so that A on the outside lines up with B on the inside, B with C, C with D, and so on. Let's say the message you want to code is 'Go to the store in five minutes.' On the outside wheel, find the letter in the message, then write down the letter that matches it on the second wheel. 'Go to the store in five minutes' becomes 'fn sn sgd rsnqd hm ehud lhmtdr.'"

"Huh!" Ismail said. "I guess bin Laden had a lot of time on his hands hiding in his compound."

"Can you give us a few minutes and we'll track you down? It shouldn't take long. I'm glad NSA didn't take time to decode this; it should be fun," Burk said, and he and Darcy started to work on the puzzle.

"Knowing those two, it won't take long," Ismail said. "What I don't get is that al Qaeda tried to hit us twice a few days ago, and only by the grace of God we took-out the three at the Cow Palace, or it would've been worse. I thought they'd be basking in their glory by now."

"That's it," Jeannie said.

"What?" Ismail replied.

"That's it! No one has taken credit for the attack at the cathedral. Al Qaeda should've been all over that--bragging to everyone who has a television set or radio. But, they haven't. They're not through.

"Those other attacks were decoys?" Ismiel asked.

"I'll bet that's exactly what they were. Look at the number of police and federal agents scouring in all fifty states, trying to anticipate if there really were going to be new al Qaeda attacks. Then we get hit at the cathedral with another attempt at the president's fundraiser, yet they're quiet." Jeannie quickly grabbed her phone and began dialing a number.

"Who are you calling?" Ismail asked.

"Pinheiro," she said.

"Hey, now's not the time for romance. We have work to do," a laughing Ismail said.

"Rick, it's Jeannie. Yeah, hi. Look--has there been more or less chatter picked up by the NSA after the two attacks on the 10th?" Jeannie asked while looking at Ismail. "That's what I thought! We just got a coded message from NSA saying that they feel there might another target here in the city. We're trying to decipher it as I speak. Wouldn't al Qaeda be burning up the Internet bragging about their success at the cathedral massacre? Instead, it's like the entire jihadist's community is expecting something bigger--don't you think?"

Before Pinheiro could answer, Darcy raced out of the elevator and shouted, "It's BART!"

"Jesus, Ricky! It's the Bay Area Rapid Transit," an excited Jeannie said. "I've got to go."

"Wait," Pinheiro said, I'm at the secret service office and I'll meet you in 20 minutes. With that he hung up.

While Darcy and Ismail waited for the elevator car to return, Jeannie knocked on Lomax's open door and shouted, "Their next target is BART!"

Holding the elevator door open with Darcy and Ismail already inside, Jeannie and Lomax climbed in. Reaching Darcy's and Burk's office, Burk had the deciphered message on the table so all could read:

America is looting the natural resources of the Muslim world, occupying the Arabian Peninsula, including the holy sites of Islam, and supporting governments servile to U.S. interests in the Middle East.

They take our oil to make fuel to drive their fancy cars. We must kill as many Americans as possible as they commute--bridges, roadways, gathering points.

From Paradise I seek revenge,
The infidels will have a watery grave.
In San Francisco they drive cars underwater.
Make this their grave.

"That has to be it. Can anyone think of somewhere else where people drive underwater?"

Lomax asked. No one had an answer, although they all processed bridges and dams--but those did not operate underwater. "OK, people. Get on it," Lomax said as he left the office.

The elevator door opened and Pinheiro exited. The first agent he saw was asked for the whereabouts of

Jeannie. The agent pointed to Darcy and Burk's office, and as Pinheiro got closer, he almost ran into both of them. "Damn, you got here fast….fifteen minutes?" Jeannie asked.

"What did you take--a DHS helicopter?" Ismail asked while hitting his cousin on the shoulder.

"Actually, the traffic was light and most of the assholes honored my red lights and siren for once. So, what do you have?"

They walked back to Darcy's and Burk's office. The crude coding device was still on the table as well as the deciphered message. Pinheiro looked at it and then turned to face everyone. "With everything else that's happened, we should've treated this as their main target all along."

Darcy was standing with Burk at a long table away from the one with the decoder. They had downloaded a substantial amount information about the BART system. "Taking the lines '*cars driving under water, make this their grave,*' we both surmise they're referring to the BART tube." Darcy said, and continued. "The Transbay Tube or BART Tube is an underwater rail tunnel running four trans-bay lines under San Francisco Bay, between us and the city of Oakland. The tube is three-point-six miles long including approaches from the nearest stations; one of which is underground. It's six-miles in length and has a maximum depth of a hundred and thirty-five feet below sea level. The tube is one of the busiest sections of the entire system in terms of passenger and train traffic. During peak commute times, over twenty-eight thousand passengers per hour travel through the tunnel.

BART trains reach their highest speeds in the tube, almost eighty-miles per hour, more than double the average of thirty-six miles per-hour speed in the remainder of the system. The tunnel's set in a trench sixty feet-wide with a gravel foundation two feet deep and is made up of fifty-seven individual sections. After the steel shell was completed, water-tight bulkheads were fitted and concrete was poured to form the two-point-three-foot thick interior walls and track bed.

The western terminus of the tube directly connects to the downtown Market Street Subway near the old Ferry Building, north of the Bay Bridge. The tube crosses under the western span of the Bay Bridge between the San Francisco Peninsula and Yerba Buena Island, and emerges in Oakland along Seventh Street, west of Interstate Eight-eighty. Here's a picture from the archive of what it looks like down below," Darcy said.

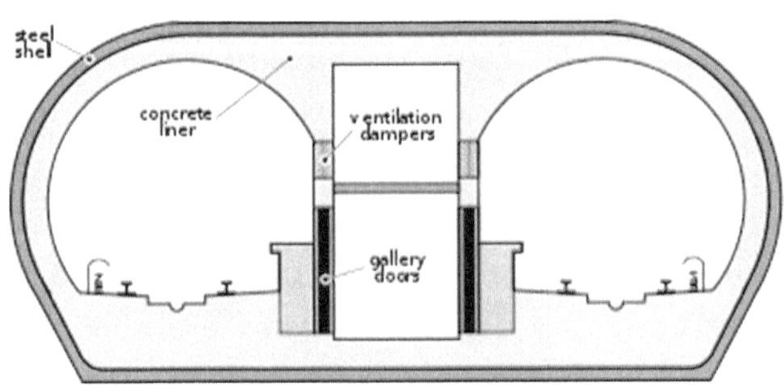

Everyone studied the picture but no one said anything for several seconds. Finally, Darcy said, "Damn, I rode BART last night."

"Gee, any ideas on how they might attack this?" asked Burk to no one in general.

"We don't have a lot of time to speculate," said Pinheiro. "Jeannie, have your team notify all BART stations that they need to be particularly vigilante and note anyone acting suspicious. Don't give them too many particulars since we don't want a panic." After dialing a number on his cellphone, Pinheiro was heard to issue more orders. "Contact the Coast Guard. See if there's been any unusual boating in the area that crosses over the Tube. Contact NSA and tell them what we suspect. Next, contact the Secretary of DHS. Fill him in about the code, and that I'm requesting at least one or more SEAL teams to be available in case we find the jihadists. We're still conducting our initial investigation to decide where on the BART system they might hit. This is urgent."

"Should we shut the system down?" Burk asked.

"I fear that after what we saw at the cathedral massacre--if they get wind that we're on to them they'll immediately commence their plan. It's a calculated risk, but I think we need to determine where they might hit, and when," answered Pinheiro.

CHAPTER THIRTY-SEVEN

MARCH 15TH

At 1600 hours Abu, Saif, and Khalid arrived at the marina. At best, they had about one-hour of usable sunlight left. Abu signed the paperwork to use the boat for an overnight cruise around the bay, paying in cash; and then he walked down to the vessel where Saif and Khalid stood with scuba gear. A heavy-duty black trash bag containing over 50-pounds of high-grade explosive sat next to the gear. In silence they loaded the gear and explosive into the boat, and after untying the mooring lines they set out to a predetermined area over the BART tube.

San Francisco Bay was extremely calm that evening--no white caps. The Kingfisher model 2525 was ideal for their purpose. It's overall 25-feet length, cabin measuring around 8-feet, and 250-horsepower engine made it possible to maneuver through the current heading out to the Golden Gate bridge, away from their target.

Abu used his cellphone to hone in on the exact coordinates of where the BART tube would enter the bay from the Mission Street entrance. He had taken several rides on the train from this station, noting his position when the train started its decent. As they got closer to land, he could see familiar landscapes where he knew the tube started. He told Saif to stop. They were over the target. Abu and Khalid began to chant prayers while taking off their clothes and climbing into their wet suits. Saif assisted them in putting on their air tanks. They were ready to enter the bay. Once overboard, Saif handed Khalid an underwater lamp and then handed the explosive to Abu. They slowly descended into the dark waters of San Francisco bay.

Saif did not hear the approaching Navy SEALs Special Warfare Combatant Crafts, and was startled when three blinding lights focused on him. He then noticed several red laser beams on his chest, and before he could react, he fell backwards with two bullet wounds in his forehead and five in his chest. The SEALSs craft advanced toward the Kingfisher. One SEAL climbed onboard, and making a motion of slashing his throat, indicated to everyone that this guy was out of the fight.

Four SEALS, already dressed in SCUBA gear, rolled off their boats armed with Mares Mini-Mini Pneumatic Spear guns. They liked the spear gun's short length, but especially its firepower. Using night vision underwater goggles, they slowly descended into the nearly black fluid. The night vision goggles gave them about 4-feet of visibility at best, and the first thing they noticed were the bubbles emanating from the jihadist's regulators. The entire incident was being heard in real-time by Jeannie and her team from a walkie talkie Pinheiro had placed on Lomax's desk.

Two of the Navy SEALs saw the two terrorists attempting to apply a type of adhesive to a long length of what appeared to be rope. They recognized that it was detonating-cord normally used to remove trees and old dock pilings. This was wrapped around the outside of a large amount of C-4 explosive. For some reason, Saif detected something behind him and turned, quickly trying to get the attention of Khalid, but it was too late. The SEALs shot their spearguns simultaneously, one hitting Saif in his facemask which instantly filled with blood. Khalid had moved slightly so the spear entered his neck, striking his carotid artery. He began to shake like a wounded fish but before he could reach for anything, the SEAL who shot him, slit his throat.

The other two SEALs each grabbed a terrorist and checked their hands. Sure enough, there were trigger devices on each of their left hands. The two shooters removed the explosives from the tube, and with an unwater marking device placed an X over the spot that had cradled the explosives. The murkiness of the water prevented them from taking photos.

Hearing the all clear signal on the walkie talkie, everyone in the room seemed relieved. For a moment, no one spoke; they just looked at each other. Jeannie locked eyes with Pinheiro and felt there was definitely a connection taking place. "OK. Well, I need to get over to the command post and check-in with the SEAL teams and my comrades. If I get further intelligence, I'll contact you sir," Pinheiro said looking at Lomax. "Also, I need to let everyone know that nothing happened tonight. There'll be no press releases, and if anything gets leaked, there'll be hell to pay; plus, you'll not believe the amount of denial that'll come out of the DHS, NSA, and the White House. It's best that the public has no idea of what we stopped tonight." He nodded towards everyone, smiled at Jeannie, and left the office. He had a long night and day ahead of him.

"OK, let's go home and get a good night's sleep. We'll reconvene and debrief tomorrow morning at nine o'clock. Good job everyone," said Lomax as he stood and started toward his hat rack. Everyone else funneled out and headed for Jeannie's office.

"How about that," Ismail said. "Three jihadists scumbags attempt to blow up the BART tube and were taken out by Navy SEALs. Yet, the public will wake up tomorrow morning with no clue as to what happened tonight." No one said anything until

Jeannie replied, "Maybe our government doesn't' feel we can handle so much bad news at one time. You know, no news is good news. Honestly, I don't know. Let's get the hell out of here. Darcy, you're not taking BART are you?" she asked.

"No way! Burk is taking me home," she replied sheepishly. The four took the elevator down to the garage, and after saying goodnight, each departed in their own direction.

Jeannie woke up to knocking on her front door. She put on her robe, and looking through her peek hole saw Delores standing on her porch. "Good morning Delores," she said, opening the door. "What's going on?"

"Hi Jeannie, I just wanted to check to see if you're OK, I mean with all of those terrorists running amok in San Francisco and at the Cow Palace--what's the world coming to?"

"There's a lot of sick people at there," Jeannie replied.

"Now that things are over, will you be able to take some time off again? We'll watch your house and take care of your garbage if you want. Just say the word," she said.

"In fact, I'll be taking off for two weeks soon, but it'll have to wait until I clear out all of the paperwork associated with the past events. I'll let you know. And oh, thank you so much for the candy." Delores got a big smile on her face and realized that the conversation was ending since Jeannie was starting to close her door.

"You're so welcome. Talk to you soon," Delores said as she retreated back to her house.

Jeannie arrived at the bureau later than everyone else. There had been a traffic accident on the Dumbarton bridge that tied up traffic in both directions. She checked-in with Tami who said everyone was waiting in the large break room versus the briefing room. When she entered, she saw Darcy, Burk, Ismail, other members of her team, and Lomax. Bagels, various flavored cream cheeses and coffee were on the table. She apologized for her tardiness while helping herself to the bagels, coffee and cheese spreads.

Lomax said that he received a phone call from Agent Pinheiro early in the morning. "In a nutshell, he said thank God for the marina manager who called and shared his suspicions about the three jihadist who tried to blow up the BART tube. The quick action of DHS and the involvement of the Navy SEALs averted a disaster of major portions. DHS and NSA were able to identify the three as Algerian nationals," he said while handing out several papers containing pictures of the three. DHS is working with the NSA to see how they got past security at their point of entry—although we may never know. Each of them had access to a suicide vest, but only this guy, Saifi, had one on.

They were staying together at a Motel 6 in Burlingame. DHS hit their rooms with search warrants and found the same stuff as the teams that hit the cathedral and the Cow Palace. What they were planning to do after setting off the explosives on the tube, we don't know. It's also unknown who sponsored them. I'll speculate--but it stays in this room--that since our country was attacked our current president will light up their world once their identity is known. Agent Pinheiro called me late last night to inform us that the chatter being monitored by the NSA has really quieted down. Al Qaeda is still bragging about the cathedral massacre, but no one is talking about the failed attempt at the president's fundraising event, nor is there any reference to BART. Alright, enjoy the bagels and cream cheese. Jeannie, when you and Flores are free, I need to see you in my office."

Jeannie and Ismail finished their bagels, and after washing them down with coffee they walked together to the SAC's office. "Unfortunately, you two will not be able to take your two weeks right now. You're both to take a red eye flight to Washington D.C. for a meeting with the president," he said, and then paused with a smile. "Apparently you two did something extraordinary and will be receiving an award from the president in the Oval Office."

CHAPTER THIRTY-EIGHT

"Good morning, Mr. President," said both Jeannie and Ismail. The president stood, walked around his desk, and gave each a warm and sincere handshake. "On behalf of a grateful nation, I can't wait to award you both with the Presidential Medal of Freedom award in a few minutes in the Rose Garden. Who knows how many lives you two saved at my fundraising event at the Cow Palace."

"Thank you, Mr. President, but it was a team effort. Our team back in San Francisco, the NSA, and DHS, all worked together to prevent what would've been as deadly an attack as the one at the cathedral," Jeannie said.

"I agree with you on that Agent Loomis, and you and your partner's modesty are admired, but I've read all of the reports from all of the agencies involved, and it was the action of you two and the DHS sniper that resolved the situation expeditiously. Then, if my information is correct, your team deciphered a note from our old past-nemesis, Osama bin Laden, who had instructed the destruction of the BART tube." He shook his head and said, "The death and destruction of that terrorist's act," he paused, "I don't even want to envision it. Thank you; thank you both." He again shook their hands and had coffee and cake brought to the Oval office where they talked about sports, the upcoming San Francisco Giants chances, as well as the 49ers.

The celebration in the Rose Garden during which both receive their Presidential Medal of Freedom lasted only thirty minutes or so, and then Jeannie and Ismail whcre driven back to the airport for a return trip home. "That was short and sweet, huh?" Ismail remarked as he looked at the black velvet box containing his award. "Looks like I'm going to have to vote for him again in November."

By the time they arrived back in San Francisco and returned to the bureau, the place was nearly deserted. Jeannie checked her messages on Tami's desk and was a little hurt to find nothing from Pinheiro. "Oh well, he's a 'Trav'lin Man' she thought. She did find a note from the SAC congratulating her on her medal and then instructing her and Ismail to start their two-week break starting the following Monday. She relayed the order to Ismail who was delighted to receive the news. They parted in the bureau garage, and each headed home.

Jeannie enjoyed the drive back over Dumbarton bridge in her Corvette. The traffic was light, so she shifted through the gears, going well over the speed limit. "Screw it," she thought, "I just got awarded the Presidential Medal of Freedom." She didn't want to hit-up Ismail for his truck to use on a possible trip to Idaho. Instead she decided to check the Internet and see what the weather and road conditions were expected to be over the next two weeks. Arriving home, she parked the Vette in her garage, but something told her to check her front door instead of going into the house from the garage. She was glad she did. On the porch she found a large Styrofoam box used for insulation. On the outside was only her name and address and the name of the company, Shari's Berries. "Damn it, Delores," she thought. "But wait a minute. What if those assholes found out where I live? This could be a bomb."

Jeannie backed away from the box and immediately called the Newark Police Department who arranged for a bomb disposal team to go to her house. Not taking any chances, Jeannie woke-up Delores as well as the neighbor on the other side of her, asking them to leave their homes until they got an all-clear. After what seemed forever, the bomb squad informed Jeannie it was just a box of strawberries and she should enjoy them.

She returned to her vehicle where she retrieved her burger and fries, expressed her apologies to her neighbors, and reached for the box. The box was heavy and awkward to carry, since she also had her purse and a bag containing a double cheeseburger and fries from an In-and-Out Burger located close to her home. "Well, at least I'll have some dessert after I finish my burger," she thought as she grabbed a knife from the kitchen and began removing the tape that kept the top and bottom of the Styrofoam box together. Removing the top of the box, she found a greeting card supplied by Shari's Berries which read, "Congratulations on your award. Thinking of you. Ricky."

MARCH 17TH

A U.S. Air Force MQ-9 Reaper drone was armed with Hellfire missiles and a 500-pound bomb in a hangar at Kandahar Airfield, Afghanistan. After the president visited CIA headquarters in the first weeks of his presidency, he toured the secure floor where agency officers direct drone strikes against suspected terrorists. Impressed by what he saw, the president conveyed to the new incoming CIA director and the assembled agency officers that he wanted them to take a more aggressive posture.

Soon afterward, the CIA began carrying out drone strikes that might not have been authorized under the Obama administration--including in Syria, where the military has taken the lead on targeting militant leaders. The White House granted CIA officers more autonomy to decide on whether and when the U.S. can pull the trigger in various places around the world, but tonight, the president would be in attendance and it was personal.

"Good morning Mr. President," said the CIA director upon the president's entrance to a large darkened room inside the Pentagon. Displayed on a large screen covering a 20 by 40-foot section of wall space, the president could view a split screen image of a United States Air Force Captain controlling a MQ-9 Reaper drone aircraft from the "cockpit" room at Kandahar Air Field in Afghanistan.

"This is their camp?" the president asked the CIA director.

"Yes, Mr. President and we have just confirmed that Ayman Baghdadi is inside the tent with several other high-ranking leaders of al Qaeda," came the reply as the CIA director pointed to an area on the right side of the screen.

"Who's in the other tents?" the president asked.

"Jihadists recruits and trainees. Everyone in this entire area hates Americans," the CIA director said, while circling the area with a laser.

The president looked back at the left portion of the screen that showed an array of computer screens displaying maps, video feeds, and gauges in front of the pilot. He intently examined the display while manipulating a joystick and throttle control, awaiting the command.

"For those you killed with your cowardly act on the soil of the United States of America, it's time for you to face your God. Take those bastards out," the president said.

The command was acknowledged by the Air Force captain who was seen maneuvering the drone over the target area. On the right screen a cross-image traveled across the terrain, approaching the tent containing Baghdadi, the al Qaeda leader.

The president and all in the room heard the pilot announce that the bomb had been released. Soon, the entire screen on the right displayed a white flash. The president could hear the Air Force captain say, "poof" while opening his closed hands replicating an explosion. As the bomb residue, debris and smoke cleared, viewers saw the entire area wiped clear of anything living or dead. All that remained was sand.

Jeannie made the drive to her cabin at Coeur d' Alene Lake in record time. After packing a picnic basket with sandwiches, snacks and drinks, she listened to her latest audiobook, *The Ark of the Covenant--Raid on the Church of Our Lady Mary of Axom,* and only stopped to use restrooms and stretch her legs on the way to Idaho. The normal sixteen-hour drive took her fourteen and a half hours, thanks to Lomax alerting the director of the Idaho State

Police that an agent, driving a red Corvette without emergency lights, would be traveling at a high rate of speed to handle a high-level federal case related to the terrorist events that happened in California. "Not too much of a stretch," she thought. She was involved in the original investigation and the aftermath of the terrorist's attacks and needed rest as a result.

An hour out from her cabin she found an all-night diner open. She pulled in and parked. There were several big rigs in the parking lot which her mom and dad always took as a sign that the food being served was good. When she walked in, she saw most of the truckers eating at the bar, talking to the only waitress on duty. She grabbed a menu and approached Jeannie. "Sit anywhere you want, honey." She then followed Jeannie to a small corner booth that could easily fit a party of six. The waitress handed her a menu and asked if she wanted coffee. Jeannie declined, but said she would like some water.

Glancing at the menu, she decided to order chicken-fried steak and mashed potatoes. Her mother made the best gravy for the steak and mashed potatoes when she made the dish for her. The waitress took her order and placed a glass of water on the table. A few of the truckers sneaked stares at her, although she thought she looked a mess from the long drive, but it did not hurt her ego.

Her attention turned from the seated truckers to the TV closest to her. The Fox News anchor was saying something about two Imams recently being killed in two separate traffic accidents, both hit and run fatalities in the San Francisco bay area. There were no leads and the police are still investigating. "Huh," she thought. "Payback is a bitch."

Her hunger satisfied, she put-off trying to find an open supermarket for supplies, figuring she could go shopping in the morning after a long sleep. A lot of the snow had melted and she encountered no problems driving her sportscar through the winding roadway to her cabin.

Jeannie lowered both windows for a brief period. Although the outside air was cold, it allowed the brisk smell of mountain evergreens to fill the cab. She drove up the driveway to the cabin and saw a vehicle she did not recognize blocking the garage. It was a new black 4 x 4 Ram Warlock pickup with an extended cab. Grabbing her purse and reaching inside, she found her Sig Sauer P226 - 9-millimeter semi-automatic and pulled it out. Not taking her eyes off the parked vehicle, she got out of the Vette and started walking towards it, shouting "FBI!" Come out with your hands in the air!"

The driver's door opened and Jeannie pointed the gun in that direction. A male began to slowly exit the truck. She could not see his face and with only moonlight to aid her, she tightened her hand on the gun.

"Let me see your other hand," she commanded. There was no response. Instead the male began to turn with something in his right hand, but it did not seem to be a weapon. There stood Pinheiro holding a large bouquet of red roses.

"Don't shoot! I'm just bringing roses," he said.

His toughest job was avoiding the nosy neighbor living next to Agent Loomis's residence. That bitch was constantly looking out her window or coming outside just to check the neighborhood. Fortunately, she left in her car. He took the opportunity to park his van displaying a local satellite dish provider on a side street and walked to Loomis' front door. She had a pretty good lock installed, but he was soon able to gain entry. Wearing gloves, he entered. There were apparently no alarms, so he proceeded to search the residence. Nothing was seen in the front room, dining room, nor kitchen; but he didn't think he would find anything of value there before he entered.

The master bedroom was neat and tidy. Someone had made the bed that morning. There were no clothes about, nor was anything left out on the bathroom sink or counter. He looked in her clothes closet and was impressed with her selection of pants suits and dresses.

Her nightstands had nothing of interest. She was reading an old Lawrence Sanders book and had several pairs of reading glasses lying next to it. In her dresser he found various shades of silk and cotton panties and bras. No sex toys. So far, nothing related to why he was there.

In what he took as a third bedroom due to its smaller size, he thought he might have hit a jackpot. There he saw a large 3-foot by 6-foot whiteboard with pictures of two individuals connected by string to a picture of a Bank of America. There were pictures of what appeared to be a sewer cannel and a tunnel. She had written names under the pictures of Two-step and Blackbeard. He realized that this must be a pending case she was working on, and not what he was looking for.

The second bedroom was set up as a bedroom for guests and looked like it had never been used. It had a twin bed, neutral colored bedspread, matching night tables and lamps, and a dresser with a quarter-length mirror. Opening doors to all the tables, he found them empty.

Satisfied with his search, he pulled out his burner phone and punched a number from memory. “Yes, I just completed the search of her house. Yes, the whole house. There’s nothing here related to what you requested. Maybe she keeps everything at the bureau. OK, I’m leaving now,” he said as he put the phone back in his pocket. He gave the house a once over to make sure he had not touched anything, or perhaps moved something out of its place. Feeling satisfied, he went back to the front door and opened it just a crack to make sure the busybody next door had not returned. She had not, so he relocking the door and left.

Look for FBI agent Jeannie Loomis in December's publication of *House of Special Purpose.*

www.ingramcontent.com/pod-product-compliance
Lightning Source LLC
Chambersburg PA
CBHW020600310726
48979CB00008B/1281/J

* 9 7 8 1 7 3 4 8 5 2 4 1 7 *